DESPERATE ASYLUM

ALSO BY FLETCHER FLORA

DESPERATE ASYLUM

FLETCHER FLORA

Includes the bonus short story "The Witness Was a Lady"

WILDSIDE PRESS

CHAPTER I

SECTION 1

Emerson Page thought about the girl waiting upstairs, and wished very much that he was up there with her. The girl's name was Edwina and Emerson's thinking of her was always pleasant and frequently glandular.

Edwina, whose name was lovingly abbreviated to Ed, was Emerson's wife, and at this moment he was wanting her very much, and he knew that she wanted him also. He regretted that this was not possible, or at least not practicable at the moment, but he consoled himself with the assurance that it would later be both.

The time was eight o'clock of a Saturday night in November. The place was the kitchen of a small restaurant and bar of distinction, of which Emerson was owner, in the town of Corinth, which was not in Greece. Emerson stepped out of the kitchen, where he had just eaten his own dinner, into the dining room, where he stopped and looked around and was conscious of a familiar warm diffusion of pride in his work and his accomplishment. It was not a large dining room, but it was relaxed and pleasant and good for the digestion. The napery was snowy. The silver and crystal caught and reflected the light from the ceiling. The woodwork was fine walnut, shining softly as satin. On the beige carpet from wall to wall, the footsteps of patrons and waitresses fell without sound. It was a nice room, and he had raised it like an only child from a short-order diner, and he was very proud.

Moving slowly, he skirted the room, nodding and smiling to guests at dinner, and turned under an arch into the bar. Here, light had been reduced even more than in the dining room, and he stood for a moment just inside the archway while the pupils of his eyes dilated in adjustment. A couple of men occupied stools. At a table in the rear, a man and a woman were drinking Manhattans. The woman reached over and lifted the cherry by its stem from the man's glass. The man said something and the woman laughed, putting the cherry daintily between white teeth. Beyond the man and the woman, in an automatic coin machine with its volume carefully modulated, a platter was spinning out under a needle the reproduction of a throaty female voice: *Let me go, let me go, let me go, lover.*

He listened to the voice, still thinking of Ed, and he knew that he would never want *her* to let him go. Never in the world. Thinking of her, he could see her. Upstairs in the apartment, as he had recently left her, wearing the red velvet toreador pants that were enough to excite the bull in any normal male. Curled up in the biggest chair in the room under a reading lamp, concentrating with childish intensity on one of her interminable books. Books were an obsession with her. Books on history and art and literature and all such heavy stuff as that. Even books on psychology. Stuff about what made you do things. Her hunger to know things was created by an early and deeply instilled feeling of inadequacy that was a result of her never having finished high school.

"My God," he'd said, "that was a long time ago. By now you probably know more than half the God-damn college professors in the country."

"Well," she'd answered, "after a while I may know more than the other half. Only I don't. Know more than almost anyone, I mean. I have such a hell of a time remembering the stuff. It makes me simply furious."

He stood very quietly, thinking and smiling, hoping that she would come down to have a drink with him before the night was gone. They would have a martini apiece, maybe two or three, and then they would go upstairs together, and it would be very wonderful, as it always was. It was a fine thing to have a wife you kept right on loving and wanting. It was a fine, lucky thing, and it didn't happen to every man.

Walking across the room, he crawled onto a stool at the lower end of the bar where it curved around to the wall. Roscoe Dooley, the bartender, came down on the inside and said, "Good-evening, Em. Drink?"

Roscoe was more than an employee. He was an old friend. Even more than that. Emerson thought of him as an early benefactor, one of the people on Earth to whom he owed something. Time was, as a matter of fact, when their positions had been reversed. Roscoe had been the employer, Emerson the employee. But that was a long time ago, or seemed like a long time, before the second World War, in another world. Roscoe had then owned an owl diner across town near the high school. He had given Emerson a job and had sometimes read poetry to him.

In response to the question, Emerson shook his head. "No, thanks, Roscoe. It's too early."

Roscoe looked past him through the archway into the room of damask and silver and shining crystal where people talked softly and walked soundlessly and fed themselves well.

"It looks like a good night," he said.

"Saturdays are always good."

"It's a long way from the old diner."

"Quite a way."

"I think a lot about then. How it was and everything."

"So do I."

"You were a smart kid. Quiet and smart. I always knew you were going someplace."

"I haven't gone much of anyplace, Roscoe. Just a restaurant and bar downtown."

He didn't really feel that way about it. It was a violation of his pride in what he had wanted to do and had done, and it pleased him to hear Roscoe deny it.

"It's a fine place. It's got character."

"Say it again, Roscoe. You're good for me. You're good for my ego."

"It's true, anyhow. Almost anyone could operate a place to eat and drink. A lousy filling station. It takes someone like you to give a place the kind of character you've given this place. I couldn't have done it. Not ever. I stayed out in the old diner for almost twenty years, and I'd still be there if you hadn't come and got me out and given me this job."

"It's Ed's character, not mine. I probably wouldn't be here myself if it hadn't been for her."

Roscoe's face got soft. He loved Ed in a way that went with his age. It made him happy to look at her and smell her and maybe touch her fingers when he handed her a drink.

"She's a sweet girl," he said. "I'm glad you married. Ed."

"You should have married a girl like Ed yourself."

"Me? Why the hell would a girl like Ed want to marry someone like me? I'm just a bum. Besides, there weren't any girls like Ed when I was young enough to be interested, and I've never seen another one like her since then, either."

Roscoe was in one of his gloomy periods. He was looking back and wishing things had been different for him. Emerson tried to think of something to say, but he couldn't, and just then a patron got onto a stool down the line, so it wasn't necessary to keep on trying. Roscoe went to get the order, and Emerson slipped off his stool and walked up to the big front window. He drew the drapes apart a little and stood looking out into the street.

It had begun to snow. Great flakes descended lazily from darkness into the light of the street lamps and shop windows to make a thin, white cover for this street of Corinth. Watching the slow and silent transformation of his town, Emerson felt his quiet happiness swell within him and become for a moment an enjoyable pain. He had lived all his life in

Corinth and would not have considered living anyplace else. He liked the town, and the town liked him, and he had been successful in it. Not that everything had come easily. His father had died when he was very young, leaving enough insurance to pay for a funeral and retire a small mortgage on a house that was getting old and hadn't been much when it was new, and Emerson started earlier than most boys to work at odd jobs. He delivered the local paper, *The Corinth Reporter*, and when he was finally able to buy a bicycle he began delivering parcels for various small merchants who didn't have enough business to maintain a regular service.

At the age of sixteen, the year before the war began, he got a job working in an owl diner from six to midnight. This was the diner owned by Roscoe Dooley, a man of unsuspected sensitivity and compassion. He felt that he had lost his way in life, and this had created in him a kind of gentle resignation instead of the bitterness that often comes to people who feel that way. He didn't have much of anything to do in the evenings after Emerson relieved him in the diner, and so he often stayed on until nine or ten o'clock, sitting in a canvas lawn chair behind the counter and reading the poetry of Edwin Arlington Robinson. Sometimes, when there were no customers on the little stools on the other side, he read some of the poetry aloud to Emerson. Emerson thought the poetry was very beautiful, especially the way Roscoe read it, but he couldn't understand why anyone should feel as bad about everything as this Robinson did...

Emerson liked his job in the diner, and he began to think about having a diner of his own. He was very good with food, and after a while Roscoe began to let him make a few changes in a menu that hadn't changed in ten years, except that the chili was omitted when the weather got hot. He began to save a little money, though not much, and he had it all planned how he would buy an old coach from the railroad and fix it up with booths and have it moved onto a spot of ground where the trade would be good. But all this was spoiled by the war. While he was in the army, his mother died and he came home briefly on leave to see her buried beside the father he could hardly remember, and there was no time, as there never was in those days, for more than a gesture of mourning, the slightest concession to grief. To tell tie truth, his mother had been a tired, morose woman for many years, and he had admired her courage and respected her position, but had never loved her greatly.

Two years later, on the island of Leyte, he was hit in the right leg by a machinegun bullet while he was going up the slope of a ridge one wet, gray dawn. The bone was broken, and while he lay patiently in the rain until a medic could get to him, the mortar platoon that was supporting the attack from the rear dropped half a dozen short rounds on their own men, which was something that happened more often than is generally admitted, and he picked up a couple pieces of shrapnel in addition to the bullet, one of which broke the same leg in another place. He was left with a bad limp, but in compensation for this he was released early from the army and received a small pension.

Back in Corinth, he sold the house his mother had left and got much more for it than he had expected because of the inflated value of real estate. With the money from the house to invest and the pension to help carry him through the hard time of getting started, he was able to do a little better than an old railway coach. He rented a narrow building next door to a bowling alley and opened a diner. He served only short-orders, but the food was good, and maybe he got some breaks besides, but for whatever reasons there were, he did well and made some money. And all the time he kept thinking about the kind of place he really wanted to own, a small restaurant and bar of distinction where good people came for good food and good drinks. A place of integrity, he called it in his mind.

It was not long before there was more work than he could do by himself in the diner next door to the bowling alley. He had a boy who washed dishes, but he needed someone to help him with the short-orders behind the counter and to serve the four booths along the opposite wall, and he decided that it would be good for business to have a pretty girl. He put an ad in *The Reporter*, and half a dozen girls answered it, but the last two were wasting their time, because the fourth was Edwina, and she was just what he wanted. As a waitress, of course. That was what he kept telling himself, anyhow, and he honestly tried to convince himself that it was true. But after a while, in spite of his efforts, he had to admit that he also wanted her another way, and a little while after that he had her. It happened in the diner one night after the dishwasher was gone and the door was locked, and it was a thoroughly co-operative and satisfactory performance.

After it was over, he drew two cups of coffee and handed her one. He was pleasantly surprised to see that she looked as good to him now as she had before, which was something that had never been true with anyone else at any other time. She took the cup of coffee and set it down and combed fingers through dark hair that was thick and almost straight, curling only a little at the ends. She wore it pretty long then, almost to the shoulders, which was the fashion. Her white uniform, re-donned, fitted her slender body snugly.

"I'll get the cream out of the refrigerator," she said.

"I'm sorry," he said. "I forgot you use cream."

She got the cream and put some in her coffee. She used a lot of it. The color of the coffee after the cream was in it, he noticed, was almost exactly the same color as her skin.

"I shouldn't have done that," he said.

"Done what?"

"You know. What I just got through doing."

"It wasn't you. It was us."

"It was my fault, though. I started it."

"Did you? That's what men always think."

"I've been trying not to do it. The trouble is, you're so damn pretty."

"Thank you. Have you really wanted to before?"

"Lots of times."

"Why haven't you, then?"

"Because you're a good girl. Does that sound corny? Because I can't get married or anything for quite a while yet."

"Don't be silly. I don't expect you to marry me."

"I wouldn't blame you if you did."

"Do you think a fellow ought to marry the first girl he makes love to?"

"Well, not necessarily. This isn't my first time. I'll admit that."

"If a fellow married the first girl, I'd already be married. Would you like that?"

"No, I wouldn't. I never thought about it like that. As a matter of fact, I didn't even think about its having happened to you before."

"Well, you're pretty green for a fellow who talks so big, I must say. Couldn't you tell?"

"I guess I could have told if I'd thought about it."

"All right. Now you can quit thinking about it."

"I don't think I want to quit. You're the prettiest gill I've ever seen."

"Being pretty isn't enough. A girl has to be smart to keep a man interested."

"You're smart enough."

"No, I'm not. I'm not smart at all. I'm ignorant. *I* didn't even finish high school."

"Finishing high school doesn't make you smart. Lots of dumb kids finish high school."

"Just the same, anyone ought to finish high school, at least. I'll bet *you* finished."

"Well, I just did. I never went to college or anything. I went into the army instead."

"You could have gone after you got out. On the GI Bill."

"I didn't want to go."

"Don't you ever wish you had?"

"No. There's something else I want to do."

"What?"

"I want to have a restaurant and bar downtown. A nice place people will come to and talk about and come back to."

"That would be fun. Someday you'll have a place like that, too. Sooner than you think, maybe. May I come and work there?"

"Probably you won't even want to. Probably you'll be married to a millionaire by that time."

He drank some coffee. It had got cold, so he went over and poured it down the drain beneath the water tap and drew some hot from the urn.

"More coffee?" he said.

"No, thanks."

He carried his own cup back to where she was and set it down and let it start getting cold like the other. The flush of color was still in her cheeks that had risen there in the excitement earlier.

"Who were the others?" he said.

"Others?"

"The ones before me."

"What difference does it make? It had nothing to do with you then."

"I know. I guess I'm jealous."

"You shouldn't be. If you'd been there, it wouldn't have happened. Except with you, I mean. Anyhow, it wasn't others. It was just other."

"That doesn't make me feel any better. It makes him sound like someone special, whoever he was."

"I thought he was special, but it turned out he wasn't."

"What happened to him?"

"It was during the war. He went into the army and didn't come back."

"Killed?"

"No. I don't think so. He just didn't come back."

"Were you sorry?"

"I was glad. I didn't want him to get killed, but I didn't want him to come back, either."

He picked up his cup and hers and carried them to the sink.

"I'll take you home," he said.

"You don't have to. I can go alone."

"I want to do it."

"All right. If you really want to."

She lived with her mother in a house that was about two miles from the diner, and he said he would get a taxi, but she said she would rather walk, so they did. At the house it happened again, and it hadn't lost anything, and afterward he walked back to town to his own room and sat there thinking about her. He looked down from his window into the street and watched a policeman walk slowly along the other side. The policeman stopped to rattle the door of each shop to see if it was locked, and after he had passed, the street was empty for a long time. Then there was a drunk who got too close to the curb and slipped off and fell in the gutter and got up and stayed in the gutter and walked carefully to the corner and out of sight across the intersection. The street was empty again for a while, after which there was a taxi going one way and a milk truck going the other, and by that time Emerson had decided that he would marry Edwina, not because of what they had done, because he felt like he had to, but just because it was something he wanted.

The next day when she came to work he told her. "Are you sure?" she said.

"Yes, I'm sure."

"Why?"

"Because I love you. I thought about you all night, and it hurt, and I kept wanting you."

"Still? Even after—?"

"Yes."

"I'm glad."

"Was it the same with you?"

"It's the same with everyone when they're in love."

"I can't understand how it happened to you. With a guy like me. You could get almost anyone if you tried."

"Well, silly, I don't want almost anyone. I want you."

"But why?"

"I don't want to pick it apart. Maybe because you're a shrewd guy who will have a nice restaurant and bar downtown that people will go to and talk about and go back to. Maybe because you've got a funny, ugly face that makes me feel excited. I wish I were smarter. I wish I had gone to high school and even college. Then people would say what a brilliant wife Emerson Page has. Everyone would say what a lucky fellow Emerson Page is to have a wife like that."

"That's what they'll say anyhow. They see what you look like, they won't care if you've ever been through high school, or any school at all."

"No, really. I want to know things. I think everyone has a kind of obligation to read books and develop his intelligence and all that, don't you?"

He hadn't thought about it at all, but he said he agreed with her. He thought she was very cute when she talked like that. Now that he had made up his mind, he wanted to get married right away.

"Let's close the diner and go down to the City Hall and get a license," he said.

"Do you really want to? Don't you want to think about it? It would be all right if you changed your mind."

"No, I don't want to think about it anymore. I want to get married."

"We'll have to wait three days. It's the law."

"The hell it is! Why?"

"We'll have to take blood tests and things. You got anything catching, honey?"

"Not that I know of. You never can tell, of course, with a wild guy like me."

"Oh, sure. You're wild, all right. You couldn't even tell about me."

"Well, I thought you were decent. You know how some girls can fool a guy. How the hell was I supposed to know you were promiscuous?"

"Listen. You sound like someone who's changing his mind. Maybe we'd better hurry down to City Hall and get that license before you talk yourself out of it."

"I'm not going to talk myself out of anything."

"All right, then. Let's go."

They did. They locked the diner and went down to the City Hall and got a license and waited three days and got married. After that they found a large room with a bath above a clothing store for forty dollars a month and moved into it, and everything was remarkably wonderful, and neither of them regretted what they had done or wished for a minute that they hadn't done it. From the bed in the room, they could read the neon identification of a shabby funeral parlor across the street, and they sometimes lay there quietly and talked about dying, and how it would be to be dead, and how neither of them would want to live without the other now that they knew what having each other was like. Beyond the funeral parlor in the sky, they could see the brighter wash of light from the better downtown area, and they talked about the restaurant and bar they would have there, the place of integrity, and he began to understand after a while that her mind was much more daring and decisive than his.

"How much money do you have?" she said.

"A couple thousand," he answered.

"All right. Take the two thousand. You've never used your loan rights under the GI Bill. Add that. We could mortgage the house my mother's living in. It belongs to her, of course, but she'd borrow on it if I asked her. Add that. It would come to something, honey. A lot of money. What I mean is, why wait? We could have the place right now. Right now, Em!"

Her voice in talking about it acquired a desperate urgency, as if they might die tomorrow and lose all of their chances forever, and it frightened him a little.

"I don't know, Ed. Maybe it's too soon."

"It's not too soon! It's not, it's not!"

"We'd need a lot of luck."

"Sure, we would. And we'd get it. Our kind of luck, Em. Good luck."

She was irresistible, so they finally did it, and they had the luck. They found the building in the place they wanted, and they sank over ten grand in it right away, and people came to it and came back, and every year they sank more and made it better, and it made money for them and made them happy, and at last they had it securely, and, best of all, they had each other and would go right on having each other until it was time to find out how it was to be dead.

* * * *

And now, at this time in the place of integrity, he stood at the window and watched the snow falling, and remembered all these things that had happened, and saw Avery Lawes get out of his black Caddy at the curb and cross the sidewalk to the door.

SECTION 2

Letting the drapes fall together across his view of the street, he turned and watched Avery come through the door and shake the snow from his hat. He had known Avery for as long as he could remember, as one boy is likely to know another in a town of thirty thousand. Avery was the last of the Laweses, the first family of Corinth since the beginning of Time—which was, in the minds of those who cared, the beginning of Corinth—and he lived now, as the family had always lived, in a big house of red brick on High Street above the river. In spite of social position, however, Avery had always been a pretty good kid by the standards of kids. He had gone to public school like the others, had always been rather shy and withdrawn, displaying sometimes an appealing eagerness to be liked and accepted. A handsome boy, he was now a handsome man, slender and graceful, as if he'd been specially tutored in the proper way to hold himself and to walk and to gesture restrainedly with his hands. He talked slowly and precisely and softly because of an impediment in his speech which showed up to embarrass him if he got careless.

People in Corinth wondered when Avery would get married. Ambitious mothers with eligible daughters were especially concerned, and most of the daughters themselves would have been happy to sign a contract to share his four-poster. He had, they felt, a moral obligation to procreate that was beyond the ordinary. Alone now, the only surviving Lawes, he held the family name in toto on the dark brink of extinction. And he wasn't getting any younger. He was Emerson's age, thirty; not that Avery seemed to be worried about it, or even conscious of it in any way of special significance. He was seldom in the company of women, or any company at all, and though he had acquired, since the death of his father in late summer, the habit of coming in Emerson's place two or three times a week for dinner and at odd times for drinks at the bar, he was invariably alone.

Watching him hang his coat and hat on the rack by the door and move toward the bar, Emerson had a faint, fleeting impression of something read or heard, something almost remembered but not quite. A word, a phrase, a voice in his brain like a whisper. He stood quietly by the window and tried to bring it back, and slowly it came, or they came, the time and the place and the voice and its words. The old diner in the old days, and Roscoe reading Robinson behind the counter. Reading aloud the brief and beautiful fragment in rhyme that told how a man had gone home one night and shot himself. A man named Richard Cory. A man imperially slim. That was the phrase. Imperially slim. Those were the words heard from then to now because of Avery Lawes. Seeing Avery move and take a stool and speak to Roscoe, he thought that they fitted well.

Roscoe put ice in a glass and poured Scotch over the ice. Avery lifted the glass and drank. Emerson left the window and walked over to Avery and sat down on the stool beside him.

"Good evening, Mr. Lawes."

Avery turned his head and smiled. "Hello, Em. What's with the mister?"

"Just standard propriety."

"Nuts. Have a drink?"

"Thanks. They're on the house, though. Bourbon, Roscoe."

Roscoe supplied the bourbon and went away. The good whiskey, undiluted, was mellow on the tongue, the warmth of it creeping centrifugally from the stomach. The first drink is always the best, Emerson thought, and with the thought was the awareness that it was not, with Avery, the first. Nor, probably, the second or third. His voice and movement had the carefully contained quality that is evidence of deliberate control, and there was a laxness in his mouth, a thin fog in his eyes. Lifting his glass again, he drained it and sat looking down at the uncovered cubes.

"You've got a nice place, Em," he said. "You're a lucky guy."

"Me? Well, I guess so. I guess I've had my share of luck. Compared to a lot who have had less, that is. Not compared to you, though. I shouldn't think you'd be impressed."

"Why not? You've done something, at least. I've never done anything. Maybe it's because I've never felt the necessity of doing anything."

"Is that bad?"

"Oh, I know." Avery laughed and beckoned Roscoe. "I sound like a God-damn soap opera or something. Poor little rich boy and all that crap. Well, it's not the money. Money's a pretty damn handy thing to have, and It'll admit it. Another drink? On me this time."

"I haven't finished this one yet."

"Well, finish it and have another. Two of the same, Roscoe."

Roscoe glanced at Emerson and received a nod. He filled the order and went away again. All but two of the stools at the bar were now occupied, and a girl had come in from the dining room to handle the tables and booths. The couple who had been drinking Manhattans were still drinking them. The woman had lined up cherry stems in a little row on the table to keep account of the number, and now she counted the stems and laughed, touching each stem with a fingertip and looking up and across at her escort slyly through her lashes. Watching her reflection in the mirror behind the bar, Emerson could see that she was quite drunk and would be more so but would probably not be offensive about it. The man, he thought, was probably in for an interesting evening.

He finished his first bourbon and worked a little on his second. The rocks, he noticed, were already out of the Scotch. Avery was looking at them as if he were wondering what had caused them to emerge so quickly. Emerson considered suggesting that Avery take it easy and decided that it was not his business. You could never tell how someone, even a gentleman like Avery, would react to something like that. Men were often sensitive about their capacity. But perhaps it would be possible to make the suggestion indirectly, in a way that would not be obvious.

"Snowing pretty hard," he said. "Supposed to get about four inches, I understand. That much in the streets will make driving pretty tough."

"Maybe. Forecasters are wrong half the time. You can't rely on them."

"That's true, all right. At least it seems like it. I guess you just remember the times they were wrong, though, and forget about all the times they were right."

"Wrong half the time. Absolutely can't rely on them."

"Well, it looks now as if this might be one of the times they'll hit it. I was looking out the window when you came in, and it was coming down pretty good then."

"Yes. I hate snow. Hate the cold. Hate the cold, dark winter. I'm just like a God-damn something or other. Don't know just what I mean. Something that becomes like whatever's around it. The environment. The weather and everything. Too damn sensitive. Day's cold and dark, so am I. Inside, I mean. Come to think of it, however, I'm pretty damn cold and dark inside even if the day isn't."

"Oh, come off it. You're just feeling lousy about something."

"Indigestion, maybe? Something I ate? Well, you're wrong. It couldn't be that because I haven't eaten anything. Just been drinking. Off and on, sort of. I got up this morning, and the thought came into my head. This would be a good day to drink, I thought. So I have been. Scotch. Never mix it. Just Scotch."

"You don't look like you'd been drinking all day."

"Not like a tramp? That's the Lawes in me. A Lawes always keeps up appearances. Part of the creed. Drilled into us from the cradle. You remember when I was a kid? When we were in school together? Tell me. What did you think of me then? Straight. Really what you thought."

"Well, I thought you were a pretty good kid. Not snotty like a rich kid might be. Well, just a pretty good kid, I mean, just like the rest of us."

"Wrong again. I wasn't a pretty good kid at all. Not like the rest of you. Not like any good kid that ever lived. Truth is, I was a nasty little bastard. All screwed up. Deceptive as hell. Appearances. The God-damn Lawes in me. You believe that?"

"All I can say is, you certainly didn't seem that way to me.

"Of course not. I told you. Never seem like you really are. It's the creed. I was a nasty kid, I tell you. A perfectly foul kid. Still am, of course. Not a kid, but perfectly foul. All screwed up. You don't grow out of a thing like that. It just grows with you. Gets bigger to fit. You like another bourbon?"

"No, thanks. I think I'll just work on this one awhile."

"Think I'll have another. Scotch. Soon as Roscoe gets time. Busy tonight. Cold, dark night. Snowing. Everyone drinking to keep out the cold. Roscoe won't look, damn it. Too busy."

"Never mind. I'll get it for you."

Emerson went around behind the bar and put ice cubes in a clean glass and poured Scotch over them and pushed the glass across the bar. He wished Avery would quit talking the way he was. Ordinarily Avery was a very reticent guy, but the Scotch had let his inhibitions down, and if he remembered later the things he'd said, he'd be embarrassed as hell and would feel uneasy the next time he and Emerson met, and maybe he'd just quit coming into the restaurant and bar at all. Emerson wouldn't like that Not just because of the loss of patronage, the profit. He liked

Avery, really, and he wanted him to keep on coming in and enjoying himself. That was the biggest satisfaction in running a place like this. It sounded phony, but it was true.

He went back around to his stool and got on.

"You ever been to Miami?" Avery said.

"No. Up till recently, I never had the money. Now I've got the money, I don't have the time."

"It's warm in Miami. Sun shining on the beach. Not cold and dark. Not snowing. You ever lie on the beach in the sun and feel like something was boiling out of you? All the poison inside seeping out your pores. Like creosote out of a railroad tie in the summer. Remember that from when I was a kid. Nasty little bastard. You had the feeling?"

"The only feeling I ever had on any beach was fear. In the war. Except for those times, I've never been on a beach. We'll have to take time for Miami one of these days; Ed and I."

"You ought to do it. Come with me if you want to. But I don't suppose you would. Of course not. Why should you?"

"You going to Miami?"

"Tomorrow. Driving down in the Caddy. Going tomorrow."

"Some guys have all the luck, lying around on a sunny beach while the rest of us are wading through snow."

"Got to go. Got to get myself cleaned out. Now or never. Realize it now."

"Well, it ought to be fun."

"Not going for fun. For therapy. What they call it. Nasty damn word."

"How long you going to stay?"

"In Miami? Don't know. Going on someplace from there, I think. Thinking of Havana. Never been there. Probably Mexico City, though. Store the Caddy and fly. You ever been to Mexico City?"

"No."

"I was there once. Long time ago. Went with my mother and father. Just a little kid. All I can remember is Chapultepec Park. Odd about that. Can't remember anything else, but I can remember all sorts of things about Chapultepec Park. Vendors. Hundreds of them. Selling all sorts of things. Balloons and colored bottles. Stuff to eat. Fruit, cheese, all kinds of nuts. Coconuts all over the place. Thin cakes you ate with some kind of hot seasoning. Pepper sauce, I guess. Hot as fire. Big lake there. Lots of cypress trees. And a castle. Chapultepec Castle. Man who would draw your picture in charcoal for a few cents. Artist. Probably lots of them around, but I only remember this one. He did a picture of me. Squat, dark man with a long mustache that stuck straight out to the sides. Must have been ten inches from tip to tip. Pocked skin. Ugly devil, to be truthful about it. I've still got the picture at home. The one he drew. Not very good, really."

"You remember a hell of a lot, if you ask me."

"Just about Chapultepec Park. Nothing else. We didn't stay long. My mother went to bed with a Mexican musician, and my father brought us home. I didn't know about the musician until later. Much later. Wondered at the time why the old man brought us home in such a hell of a hurry."

Emerson was startled. He remembered Avery's mother, a tall woman with golden hair who had died young. It had been long ago that she died, and his remembrance of her had lasted only because of her great beauty. She had seemed to him proud and arrogant. He couldn't imagine her going to bed with a Mexican musician or with anyone else for pleasure. He wondered if Avery could be making it up. Maybe too much Scotch made a liar of him. It was hard to believe of Avery, but you had to admit that too much to drink sometimes did odd things to unlikely people.

He got off the stool and put a hand for a second on Avery's arm.

"Excuse me," he said. "I think I'd better float awhile."

"Of course. Business first. See you later, Em."

"Sure."

"That trip to Miami. You and Ed riding along, I mean. Really meant it, you know."

"Thanks, Avery. We couldn't possibly make it, though."

"No. Thought not. Well, better go float, Em. Duty of proprietor."

"That's right. And thanks just the same about Miami." He walked up to the front window and looked out into the street again. It was still snowing, and a wind had come up. The flakes no longer drifted through the light lazily, but were driven through on a tangent, and the snow already lying on the pavement was whipped up by the wind in thin, swirling clouds. A car passed slowly with flapping wipers. Avery's black Caddy at the curb, facing into the wind, had acquired a drift against the windshield. It looked like they would get their four inches at least. Maybe more.

* * * *

Emerson turned and walked into the dining room and through the dining room into the kitchen. They were almost finished serving in the dining room, and in the kitchen they were cleaning and polishing and getting ready to wrap it up for the night. Looking at his watch, he saw that it was a few minutes after ten. He wondered if Ed would come down for the drink. He hadn't suggested it when he'd left her, and now he wished that he had. He wanted her to come very badly, and his need for her seemed to have something to do with Avery's quiet drunkenness, but he couldn't understand why that should be. He didn't want to go on thinking about Avery, but he couldn't help it. The truth seemed to be that Avery was very lonely and very unhappy about something. It was even more than unhappiness, really. A kind of despair. Sometimes a guy really gave himself away when whiskey let his inhibitions down. Sometimes you found out things that surprised the hell out of you. The truth was, it was a little disturbing. It made you wonder how much you really knew about anyone, even people you saw all the time, day in and day out, and you got the crazy idea that everyone was actually a God-damn stranger or something. Take that crack about his mother and the Mexican musician. That was a hell of a thing for a guy like Avery to come out with. Sober, he'd have cut his tongue out first.

Where was Ed? He was willing to bet, thinking about it, that she'd gone to sleep over her book. She did that lots of times. Lots of times he went up and found her curled up under the reading lamp in the big chair with the book open in her lap or sometimes on the floor where it had fallen. She was cute as all hell when she went to sleep that way. He always kissed her awake, and that usually got something bigger started. He had a notice to go up and get something started right now but decided that first he'd probably better make another tour of the bar, just to be sure everything was going along all right. Come to think of it, he'd just have Roscoe mix up a shaker of martinis to carry upstairs with him.

In the bar, trade was brisk and would stay brisk until midnight, when they would have to close because of the Sunday closing law. The man and woman drinking Manhattans were still at it, but Emerson could see by the cherry stems that they had reduced their rate of consumption. The row of stems was not much longer than it had been the last time he looked. The woman was fuzzy in the eyes and her lipstick was a little smeared but her gestures were controlled and she seemed to be talking coherently to the man across from her. No potential disturbance there. She could hold what she took, no question about that.

Moving his eyes right, he saw Avery Lawes lift his glass and drain it and stand up abruptly. Turning, Avery walked carefully toward the rack where he'd left his coat and hat. His slim body was erect and graceful in its motion. If there had been a chalk line on the carpet, he would have been on it every step. When he was abreast, Emerson stepped forward and intercepted him.

"Leaving, Avery?"

"Yes. Going home. Red brick house on High Street. View of the river and everything. Money street. Class street. Home of the Laweses, the God-damn Laweses."

"You sure you're all right?"

"Perfectly. Perfectly sober. A Lawes never gets drunk. In public, that is. It's against the creed."

"I don't know. The streets are getting bad. Looks like the forecasters hit this one."

"Really? Unusual. Never would have believed it. Fellows are usually unreliable."

"Maybe I ought to call a taxi for you. I'd be glad to run the Caddy out to your home in the morning."

"Thanks, Em. Damn gracious for you to be concerned. Won't do, though. Leaving for Miami in the morning. Early. Remember I told you?" He stopped and looked at Emerson as if he were trying to make a decision about something. "Wouldn't want to smash up the Caddy tonight, though. Spoil everything. Delay my leaving. Wonder if you'd mind running me out now. Damn gutty of me to ask. Appreciate it, however. Consider it a great favor. Get a cab out there to get you back."

Emerson didn't want to do it. He had Ed on his mind, and he wanted to get up to her right away, but he didn't know how to refuse Avery. He had a feeling, moreover, that Avery had no real doubt about his own ability to handle the Caddy in the snow. His request was based more on an urgent desire to prolong companionship, on a deep dread, perhaps, of returning alone in the cold, dark night to the old house on High Street above the river.

"All right," he said reluctantly. "But first I think I'd better tell Ed where I'm going. Besides, I'll have to get a hat and overcoat. Tell you what. You wait for me here, and I'll be as quick as I can. Okay?"

"Sure. I'll just have another Scotch while I'm waiting." Exercising the control which the Scotch made consciously deliberate but did not destroy, he walked back to the stool at the bar and got on. Emerson followed and went around behind. Roscoe was busy at the far end, so Emerson poured Avery's Scotch and mixed the shaker of martinis to carry up to Ed. With him gone, she would not want to come downstairs, and she would probably like to have the martinis while she was waiting for him to return. Cursing his bad luck and regretting his role of Samaritan, he carried the frosty shaker out through the dining room into the kitchen and upstairs from the kitchen to the second floor. Opening the door to the living room of the apartment, he saw that he had been right. Ed was asleep in her chair.

He closed the door quietly behind him and put the shaker on a coffee table and stood watching her, his heart swelling and aching, and he wondered how it was that a man could love someone so long and so hard without becoming worn out from it. She hadn't changed much since the day she'd come to work for him in the direr beside the bowling alley, except that she was a litle sleeker, a little more finished and polished by the things that money brought, and now her dark hair was not long, as it had been then, but very short in the Italian style. In the chair under the light, her knees were drawn up against her breasts, the red velvet stretched tight as second skin over the flank of the leg on his side, and her head had fallen forward until her forehead lacked only a little of touching her knees. Her lips were slightly parted and quivered with the passage of her breath. Her book was on the floor. It was, he noticed, *The Magic Mountain*.

Walking over to her silently, he leaned down and pit his right hand on her hip and kissed her as near the mouth as he could reach. She sighed and turned her face up in her sleep, and he kissed her again, now directly on the mouth, and kept kissing her until her eyes opened and her arms came up to lock around his neck.

"Em," she whispered, arching up against him. "Darling, I've been wishing you'd come."

He laughed. "Like hell you have. You've been asleep."

"Before that. Before I went to sleep I was wishing."

"I've been thinking about you. I've been thinking about you and wanting to come back ever since I left."

"Really? Isn't it wonderful how we always wish that at the same time? Do you suppose it's like that with all the others?"

"Not like with us. We're altogether unique. We never happened before and won't ever again."

"You're a seducer, that's what you are. You always know just what to say to make a wife fall apart. Especially a dissolute wife like me who seduces easily. Darling, I'm sorry I went off to sleep. I was coming down to have a drink with you."

"I thought you might come. It doesn't matter, though, I brought up a shaker of martinis."

"Oh, you're perfect. Let me up, darling. I'll get glasses."

"No. Wait, Ed. Listen to me. I've got something else I have to do first."

"Something else? What?"

"Well, Avery Lawes is downstairs in the bar, and he's pretty drunk."

"Drunk! Avery? I don't believe it."

"He is, though. You'd never know it just to see him, and I don't suppose anyone's even aware of it, except Roscoe and me, but the streets are pretty bad with the snow and all, and, well, Avery asked me to drive him home, and I didn't know how to say no."

"Really, Em! And your lovely wife simply panting!"

"Damn it, Ed, don't rub it in. I hate it enough already. Say the word, I'll go tell him to get home any damn way he can."

"No. Of course not. It's not much to do for a man, I guess. But it does seem a little odd. His asking, that is. I didn't know you and Avery were such friends."

"We're not. I've known him from when we were kids, that's all. Tonight, like I said, he's pretty drunk, and he just got talking. You know how it is sometimes when a guy's had too much. Funny thing about him, Ed. He's a very lonely guy."

"Sure. It's the penalty he pays for having all that money."

"It's true, Ed. He's very lonely."

"All right. So he's very lonely. Go drive him home and let your wife be lonely."

"Damn it, I won't go. I'll stay right here."

"Don't be a dope, darling. I was only joking. I'll wait here and think about you until you get back."

"You sure it's all right?"

"Yes. Hurry, though."

"You can certainly count on that."

"I'll wait in bed," she said, "and drink martinis."

SECTION 3

On the ascent to High Street, the rear wheels spun and whined in the wet snow. The big Caddy crept up at a fraction of the speed registered on the panel, lurching as it gained the crest, rear end skidding in the turn left. Down the street a half block, Emerson nursed it into the circular drive to Avery's house and stopped it under a portico.

"Well," he said, "here we are."

Avery was sitting slumped in the seat beside him, his chin on his chest and his eyes closed. At the sound of Emerson's voice, he opened his eyes and sat up straight and closed his eyes again and knuckled them like a child waking in the morning.

"Already?" he said. "Must've napped. Can't tell you how much I appreciate this. Come on in. Call a cab for you. Have a drink while we're waiting."

He got out on his side of the Caddy and went up onto the front porch from the portico. At the door he dug in a pocket for a key and used it efficiently, Emerson noticed, in spite of the load of Scotch he was carrying. They went into a hall and down the hall and into a room on the right that was obviously a library. A floor lamp had been left burning at one end of the room, and there was a fire in a fireplace at the other end that created a shirting pattern of light and shadows on the floor in front of it. Avery walked down to the fireplace and dropped his hat and overcoat onto a chair and stood with his hands extended toward the fire.

"Take off your things," he said. "Fix you a drink."

"I think I'd better get the cab and get on back," Emerson said. "Thanks just the same."

"Sure. Call it for you immediately. Nasty night, however. Take the cab a while to get here. You'll have time for a drink."

Reluctantly, Emerson took off his coat and advanced to the fire. Avery went out of the room and was back in two minutes.

"Called the cab. Be here in twenty minutes. Rough estimate. Now for the drink. Still bourbon?"

"Yes, thanks."

"Scotch for me. Been drinking Scotch all day. Woke up this morning and thought it would be a damn good day for it." At a liquor cabinet he got out bottles and glasses and then turned. "No ice. Forgot about ice. I'll go out to the kitchen for some."

"Never mind. Not for me, I mean. I'd just as soon take it without."

"Really? Not just being considerate?"

"No, really."

"Good. Have mine the same."

He poured the bourbon and the Scotch and brought the bourbon to Emerson. "Here you are. Bourbon for you. Scotch for me. Bourbon for the road. Scotch for bed."

Emerson thought that he had something a hell of a lot better for bed than Scotch, if he could only get home to it, and he thought of it waiting for him and was very bitter. He drank some of the bourbon and hoped that the damn cab would arrive under the estimate.

"Cold house," Avery said. "Empty house, cold house. You know what it needs, Em? This house?"

Emerson had a decided opinion on that question. He thought he knew damn well what the house needed and what Avery needed, and it was the same thing he himself needed and ought to be having and intended to have just as soon as a lousy, creeping cab could get him to it in the cursed snow.

"A woman," he said. "You ought to get married, Avery."

Avery laughed softly and took Scotch. "Yes. Woman. Wife. Thought you'd say that. Just asked to hear you say it. What everyone's thinking. What everyone's saying. Why doesn't Avery get married? Propagate. Have kids. Last of the Laweses. Avery has no kids, no more Laweses. Wouldn't that be a God-damn crying shame?"

Emerson didn't know what to say, and so he said nothing and drank some more bourbon. Avery was looking at him with a queer intentness, and it made him uncomfortable. He wished to hell that Avery would quit.

"You know why I'm not married?" Avery said.

Emerson said he didn't. He wanted to say also that he didn't care. His indifference was not prompted by callousness, but by the thought of waiting and his urgent desire to change that condition. He could see quite plainly that Avery was a lonely guy who wanted to talk, and he was sorry for him and all that, but where in hell was the God-damn cab?

"No," Avery said. "Of course you don't know. Guy like you couldn't possibly know. Probably wouldn't believe it if you did. No insult intended. Compliment, rather. Thinks straight, feels straight. Guy like you does. Would you believe it if I told you? Why I'm not married?"

"Why not? If you said it, I'd believe it."

"I wonder. Curious about it. Want me to tell you?"

"Well, that's up to you, Avery."

"Sure. So it is. Think I will. Probably because of the Scotch. Probably regret it tomorrow. Think I'll tell you, anyhow. Just to see if you believe it. Reason is, I can't stand women. Revolted by them. All women. Every damn woman on earth. As *women*, I mean. Women all right as *people*. That's different. Women as women have special function. You know. Requires a man. Thought of it makes me sick. You believe that?"

Emerson believed it, all right, because there was no reason not to believe it if Avery said it was so, but he couldn't understand it by a long shot. With a wife like Ed, whose happy lechery was a perfect complement to his own, how could he understand something like this? It seemed to him a sickness. Now he was beginning to see Avery as not only a lonely man but a sick man, and it disturbed him and embarrassed him, and he wished fervently, not for the first time that night, that it hadn't seemed to Avery like a good day for drinking Scotch.

"I guess it would be possible to feel like that," he said.

Avery lifted his glass and tipped it and seemed surprised to discover that there was nothing in it. He looked from the glass to the bottle on the cabinet and back to the glass and then apparently forgot all about both of them.

"Woman in this house once," he said. "Long time ago. Beautiful woman. Most beautiful woman on earth. Loved her. Worshiped her. Greatest happiness just to look at her, listen to her voice, have her touch me. Then it all went to hell. All to hell. Reasons I won't bore you with. Anyhow, complete reversal. Disgusted me. Absolute revulsion. Couldn't bear to have her touch me any more, hardly to come near me. Thought of her flesh made me ill. Sickness in me, of course, kind of disease.

Realize that but can't help it. Same feeling about all women. No wife. No propagation. Last of the Laweses."

He was surely talking about his mother, and what made it so bad, Emerson thought, was that it was really the Scotch talking. And it was saying things that would later be remembered and despised, and where, where, where was the lousy, creeping cab? Take that business about the Mexican musician and the hurried return from the Mexican holiday, for instance, and now all this stuff about love and hate and everything—it was the kind of stuff a guy didn't want to hear, especially a guy with someone like Ed waiting, and all he could do was keep his mouth shut and sweat it out.

And then, at last, the cab was there in the drive, its horn blasting.

With a vast sense of relief, almost of precarious escape, Emerson went for his hat and coat. He really was sorry for Avery, and he felt a little guilty about running out on a guy who was lonely and was obviously dreading an empty house, but it was impossible to stay, would have been impossible even without the consideration of Ed, because of the things Avery was saying, and you knew damn well how it would be later about his remembering and regretting. Besides, to be truthful, it was pretty damn depressing.

"That's the cab," Emerson said. "I'd better run."

"I hear it. Pretty good time, considering. Less than twenty minutes. I'll see you to the door."

"No. Don't bother. I'll get out all right."

"You sure? Appreciate very much your driving me home. Wouldn't want you to think I don't."

"It's all right, Avery. It was nothing."

"Contrary. It was a great deal. Fine act of friendship."

"All right, Avery. Good-night."

He let himself out the front door and ran for the cab and got in. He slumped back in the seat.

* * * *

There was still business in the bar, but the dining room was deserted. He went directly through into the kitchen, which was also deserted, and up the stairs from the kitchen to the apartment. Dropping his hat and coat in the living room, he crossed over into the bedroom, and there was a small lamp burning on a table beside the bed, and sitting up in the bed was Ed with a martini, and she was wearing the blue thing, the thing like smoke that looked as if it were about to drift off her entirely.

"Such a long time you took," she said.

"I know. I'm sorry."

"I'd almost decided to invite up a sub from the bar."

"Roscoe?"

"Don't sneer at Roscoe. Roscoe I love."

"I'm not sneering at him. I love the old devil as much as you do."

"Did you get Avery delivered all right?"

"Safe and sound. He's going to Miami tomorrow."

"Really? And you feeling sorry for him? When are we going to Miami, Ed?"

"Sometime. We could go tomorrow if we wanted to. With Avery. He asked us."

"He *must* have been drunk!"

"He was drunk, all right, but I think he actually meant it. He was funny. All screwed up inside, I mean. He kept saying things it wasn't like him to say."

"What things?"

"Oh, crazy stuff. About why he never married and all. About not liking women. About how his mother slept with a Mexican musician once."

"Maybe he has a psychosis or neurosis or something."

"I wouldn't know."

"His mother, you say? Really with a Mexican musician?"

"That's what he said."

"I wonder how a Mexican musician would be."

"You wouldn't like it."

"Why? What makes you so sure?"

"Because you've been spoiled."

"Well, such conceit! Are you having trouble with that shoestring?"

"Don't get impatient, darling."

"Maybe we should go to Mexico instead of Miami. Or maybe I could run down and back by myself while you're getting that damn shoelace untied."

"I'm stalling deliberately. You're cute when you're eager."

"*I'm* perfectly calm." She tossed her head. "There's a martini left. Would you care for it?"

"No. I had a couple of bourbons at the bar and another one at Avery's."

"In that case, I'll just drink it myself."

But there wasn't time, as it turned out, for the last martini. And for the next part of the evening, all romantic propaganda to the contrary notwithstanding, there was no better place anywhere—not in Miami, not in Mexico, not anywhere on earth.

CHAPTER II

SECTION 1

The snow came down fiercely over the northern part of the state, and in Midland City, the state's metropolis, it started falling shortly after dark and continued most of the night. The temperature fell slowly but steadily all that time. Between eight and midnight, the traffic squad of the city police had reports of twenty-three minor accidents, and an alcoholic who was hardly aware of the snow, or of anything else, lay down in a doorway on the lower south side and was found dead in the morning.

In the living room of a small apartment not far from the place where the alcoholic was dying, a young woman named Lisa Sheridan stood at a window and looked down into the narrow street below, and because she was lonely and depressed and felt that there was no security on earth, she was thinking of things that had happened to her in the past, not because there was anything particularly comforting in these things but simply because they were over and done with and not presently threatening. Many of the things that had happened to her were not really so much different, in fact, from the things that had happened to many other girls, but they had had vastly different effects and had come, or were coming, to vastly different ends, and she wondered why this should be so. It was a problem she was in no way equipped to solve, and it was not so much in the expectation of coming to a solution as for the simple relief she found in keeping her mind busy that she concerned herself with it at all.

Behind her in the room, sitting sprawled in an overstaffed chair with her legs spread out in front of her and a cigarette hanging from her lips, was the woman who shared the apartment. Her name was Bella Cassidy, and she had lived most of her twenty-nine years in overt conformity with one world and in covert allegiance to another. She had black hair cut short and rather shaggy, and her face was thin and swarthy with long, narrow eyes and a thin-lipped mouth. There was a natural grace in her slender body, a kind of suggested muscular toughness that was not actually evident in weight or bulges, and there was now, besides that, a quality of wariness in her whole attitude that was oddly inconsistent with her posture. Without touching the cigarette with her fingers, she drew a cloud of smoke into her lungs and released it. Through the smoke, she stared at the back of the girl at the window.

"For God's sake, sit down," she said. "It wears me out to watch you."

The imperative nature of her words did not affect the timber of the voice in which they were spoken. She sounded as if, in spite of what she said, it really made no difference whatever to her if Lisa sat down or not. Without turning, Lisa said, "I don't want to sit down."

"All right. Stand up, then. Be as childish as you like."

"I'm not being childish."

"Oh, for Christ's sake! Can't you do anything but make denials? Denying a thing doesn't alter the truth, you know. The truth is, you've decided that everything is over between us, that I've spoiled everything, and nothing I can say will make any difference."

"How do you expect me to feel?"

"I expect you to be sensible, but I see that you won't." Lisa turned and stood with her back to the window, looking at Bella with eyes that betrayed her depression and fright. She was somewhat under average height, even for a woman, but her body was so slim and straight that she did not seem to be. Her hair was soft and fine and a very pale gold, almost silver, parted in the middle and drawn back behind her ears into a knot. There was about her, in her face and the rest of her, an effect of cold delicacy that approached frailty, and she was, in fact, within the limits imposed by the coldness and fragility, very lovely. *Pale gold against the dark glass*, thought Bella, and the words came into her mind simultaneously with a kind-of catch in her heart that was for a moment ecstatic pain, and for the duration of the moment she regretted the choice she had made and the line of action she was now following.

"Is it sensible to blackmail my own family?" Lisa said.

"Why not? They're wealthy and can afford it, and it's certainly the only way you're ever going to get anything out of them."

"I don't want anything from them. It's you who wants it."

"I want it for both of us. I told you that. It's entirely unnecessary for you to make an issue of it."

"But when it comes to a choice between me and the money, you choose the money."

"That's your fault. There is no necessity, as I said, to make a choice at all. Since you're determined that I must, however, it has now become a matter of principle. I don't choose to be a fool just because you're one."

It was not the first time Lisa had been called a fool. Another girl had called her that once, but it had been a long time ago, and it was something she did not now want to remember or to think about.

"Perhaps I'm a fool," she said, "and perhaps I am many things worse, but at least I'm not a blackmailer."

Bella shrugged and sucked her cigarette. "If it makes you feel better to call me names, go ahead."

"It doesn't make me feel better. Nothing in the world will ever make me feel better again. I'm sick and frightened, and I wish I had never met you."

"Now you're simply being dramatic."

"Blackmail is a crime. You can be sent to prison for it."

"There's no danger. Your family are cowards, like all people who think the world will end if their precious respectability is compromised. They won't risk any publicity, darling."

"Suppose they don't pay. Would you do as you threatened?"

"Tell their friends about you? I'm afraid I'd have to." Bella removed the cigarette from her mouth and crushed it in a tray and laughed shortly. "Let me tell you something, darling. You had better quit being so concerned about your family, for all they wish for you in their hearts is that you had never been born or had died before you became what you are. They hate you and can't understand you and will consider you a menace as long as you are alive, and the only hope for you and me on earth is to be found in one another and in others like us."

"Did you talk with my brother?"

"Yes. He was quite indignant."

"Carl can be very hard when he wants to be. He may go to the police."

"I tell you that he won't. The risk is too great. He said he would come here tonight with the money, and he will."

"I don't want to see him."

"Well, you'll have to reconcile yourself to it. It was part of the agreement. Apparently he wants to talk with you, and I had to promise that you would be here in order to get him to come."

"You had no right to do it."

"So you have told me at least a dozen times. You even concealed your family's wealth from me for a long time, didn't you, darling, in fear that I would be tempted do do something like this? I'm still a little angry about it. And now you have threatened to leave me and you're afraid that you must do it, even though you don't want to. Well, I will tell you something that you may not know. I will tell you that you are making me a little sick to my stomach, and perhaps I would be better off without you."

Lisa turned and looked down again into the narrow street. Her depression was now so complete and unqualified that it afforded her a kind of sickly immunity, and Bella's words, deliberately cruel, were no more than a sequence of sounds with no particular significance or effect. The snow had accumulated, she noticed, on the sill outside, and had drifted in places across the street. Looking down, aware of details with a peculiar detachment that was part of her depression, she saw a man cross under the light at the corner, leaving behind him in the snow the prints of his passing. Shoulders hunched into his overcoat collar upturned against the wind and falling snow, he came on at an angle across the street and was swallowed by the shadow of the building in which Lisa stood.

It was her brother Carl. She had not seen him or heard from him for a very long while, and now, seeing him from above against the cold white earth, she thought that he looked small and pitiable and somehow vulnerable. And she was sorry that she had brought him trouble and was now, though she didn't wish it, bringing him trouble again. A sudden nostalgia stirred in the gray stillness of her depression, an intense longing for a status long lost in a time long past, and she wondered if it would be possible to regain, not physically but mentally and emotionally, the particular point and condition in time when she had started becoming what she was instead of what she might have been. If this were possible, she thought, the person that she was might be rejected and left dead in a very real way, and the person she might have been could at last start becoming. This thought appealed to her; it was something to support her in the tense waiting for her brother's approach, and she did not release it until she heard his footsteps on the stairs outside.

Turning, she said, "It's Carl. I saw him under the light in the street."

Bella leaned forward in her chair, listening to the footsteps ascend the stairs and approach in the lull, sitting fixed through a hiatus of silence until there was a sudden knocking at the door. Then, with a sigh, she stood up. There was a surety, a fluid ease of motion in her hard body.

"Perhaps I was wrong," she said. "Perhaps he wants to save you after all."

Her voice was colored by a curious mixture of irony and anger, and she stared at Lisa intently, as if she thought Lisa's reaction might be tremendously significant. But Lisa was still supported by the despair that is acquired in the ruins of the last sanctuary, and there was no discernible reaction at all. Bella shrugged, her thin lips shaping in her dark face a smile that was decisive and cruel.

"You can go to hell," she said. "You can bloody well go to hell."

The knocking was repeated, and she went quickly to the door and opened it. Carl Sheridan, across the threshold, looked at Bella and beyond her, his eyes probing the room. He was wearing a navy blue overcoat, the shoulders frosted with snow, and he was holding a gray homburg squarely before him, much in the manner of a man standing uncovered in respect or reverence. His face was drawn stiffly over its bones. His blond hair was thinning and receding and lay limply on his skull. Lisa, seeing him from her place by the window, thought that he looked as if he had been very ill and was at this moment very tired.

Bella retreated and said, "Come in. You see that I've kept my word. Lisa is here to meet you."

Carl stepped into the room two precise paces and stopped, his eyes finding Lisa. Still holding his homburg, he stood for a moment watching her, and then he made the kind of formal little bow from the waist that he might have made in acknowledging an introduction to someone he had never seen before.

"Hello, Lisa."

"Hello, Carl," she said.

His lips worked, and she thought at first that he was trying to speak again and couldn't, but apparently it was only a kind of nervous reaction, for he turned abruptly to Bella and spoke without difficulty.

"I've brought the money. Five thousand dollars."

She walked across to a small table beside the chair in which she had been sitting and picked up a pack of cigarettes. She extracted a cigarette and dropped the pack and began tapping the cigarette on a thumb nail.

"It's what we agreed on," she said.

"Yes. Exactly. Before I give it to you, however, I want to warn you against trying this again. It won't work. You are a blackmailer, guilty of a crime, and next time I'll see that you are sent to prison. I'm prepared to accept whatever publicity you can give to this affair, and if it means trouble for Lisa, she must be prepared to accept it too."

"All right. A lecture is not necessary. I've already told you that I don't believe in making a bad thing out of a good one."

"I see. Well, then…" He released the homburg with one hand and removed a thin sheaf of bills from an inside pocket of his coat. Extending the bills, he said, "Probably you will want to count it."

"No." She shrugged her indifference. "You would hardly try to cheat me in a transaction like this. Just put it down somewhere."

He tossed the money at the chair by which she stood, and it struck the overstuffed cushion and bounced off onto the floor. Bella did not stoop to pick it up but struck a match and lit her cigarette and drew smoke into her lungs deeply. Expelling the smoke, she watched it rise and thin, and appeared to have lost all interest in what went on in the room.

"So it has come to this," Carl said. "To blackmail. To crime. Is this what you wanted, Lisa?"

He was not looking in her direction when he began talking, and Lisa was a little startled to discover that he was talking to her. She was conscious of the heaviness of his words, their almost comic ponderousness, as if he were reading lines from a bad melodrama, but she was not impelled to laugh.

"I didn't want it, Carl. The blackmail. I tried to stop it."

"But you couldn't. You've started much that you can't stop, Lisa. Is that true?"

"I guess so. I guess I've started it. Anyhow, one way or another, it has got started."

"What do you intend to do now?"

"I don't know."

"Will you stay here? With this woman?"

"No. I've only stayed this long because she said you wanted me here when you came."

"Yes. I made that stipulation. Where are you going?"

"I don't know."

"Have you any money?"

"A little. I've been working. I had a job in a shop, tut I've quit."

"Do you think you could give this up? This kind of life?"

"I don't know."

"What do you mean, you don't know?"

"It's impossible to know. I suppose there is no way to make you understand that, but it's true."

"It's difficult. I admit it. To understand this kind of thing, I mean. But I've tried. If you think I was ever able to dismiss you from my mind and forget you entirely, you're mistaken. I…I've been reading about it, books about it, and perhaps I've learned a little."

His confession touched her. She had a picture of him reading at night when he was tired and would have preferred to sleep or do something for pleasure, heavy books that actually only confused and frightened him all the more, the light of the reading lamp showing his scalp through his fine, thin hair. She wanted very badly to approach him and to touch him, but she was afraid he would be offended. Revolted, even. In her fingertips she actually had the sensation of his skin crawling away from her touch.

"Thank you," she said. "It was kind of you to do that."

"Not at all. It was not a question of kindness. I have wished more than once that you would die."

"I have wished it more than once myself."

"In that case, why haven't you tried to change?"

"It's not so simple. I don't know. I can't explain it. Perhaps it's a matter of reaching the time for it. Just the right time. I don't know why I couldn't change, any more than I know why I couldn't die. Dying would have been easier."

"Tell me. Will you leave with me tonight?"

"If you ask me. You will have to ask me."

"All right. I ask you to leave with me."

"Will you take me home?"

"No. If you have any idea of ever going home again, you had better give it up."

"Do they hate me so much?"

"Hate? I don't think it's that. They pretend that you are dead. No. More than that, really. They pretend that you never lived at all."

"Where will you take me, then?"

"That's something we'll talk about. Now you had better get ready to go. Do you have much to pack?"

"Not much that I want to take. Excuse me, please." She went into the bedroom, and got a bag from the closet and began to put things into it. During the time that she and Carl had talked, Bella had stood smoking her cigarette with obvious indifference, blowing out clouds of smoke and watching each one disperse before she blew out another. From her position, she could see through the door into the bedroom, and now she watched Lisa packing with the same air of indifference, the cigarette acquiring a long ash in her fingers. She paid no attention whatever to Carl, as if he had removed himself from the earth with the payment of the five thousand dollars, which still lay on the floor by the chair, and she said nothing until Lisa returned from the bedroom after a few minutes, wearing a coat and hat and carrying the bag. Then she spoke.

"Go, then," she said. "Go, God-damn you. I'll come spit on your grave, when you're dead."

Her attitude of indifference had seemed so genuine that the vitriolic fury in her voice was a physical shock. Not to Lisa, who had experienced it before, but to Carl. He felt cold and withered inside, and a little frightened, and immediately ashamed of the fear. Stepping forward, he took the bag from Lisa's hand and put a hand on her arm. It was the first time he had touched her for years, and it did not disturb him, though the thought of ever touching her again had disturbed him many times.

They went downstairs and outside into the street. She was acutely conscious of his hand on her arm and was exorbitantly grateful for it. The wind in the street was quite strong and very cold. She was grateful for the wind too. It cut through her coat and inner clothing and was like an astringent on her skin. She lifted her face into the wet snow.

"I left the car a block over," Carl said. "The grade to this street is rather slick, so I didn't try it."

They walked to the corner and turned right across the intersection and under the light which had first shown him to her as she looked down from the window. In the car at the foot of the grade, he turned on the heater at once. The air sucked in by the fan was still warm, and she regretted this and wished that he had left the heater off, because the cold acted upon her as a kind of scourge, as the whip is a scourge to the flagellant, lifting her depression a little and easing the burden of her guilt.

"Where are we going?" she said.

"To a hotel. I'll leave you there for a day or two and come back for you later."

"What then?"

"I've been ill with pneumonia. The doctor has recommended a few weeks in the sun, and I've decided to go to Miami. Would you like to come with me?"

"If you want me to."

"That's settled, then. You needn't make any preparations. I'll take care of reservations, and you can buy clothing there."

She was overwhelmed by his kindness. She had thought that he would surely never speak to her again, or recognize her in any way, and now he had come out into the cold and snowy night to help her and was offering to take her with him to Miami. Her eyes felt hot and her throat constricted, and she was on the verge of crying, which would have been a good thing, but it had been so long since she had cried that she seemed to have lost the capacity for it.

"Thank you," she said, and could find nothing to add. Exercising excessive caution on the snow-covered streets, he drove slowly to a small hotel in a quiet section of town, and they went together into the warm, drab lobby where an old man sat facing the window and the night, and another dozed in a chair beside a rubber plant, an evening newspaper unfolded across his lap. Carrying Lisa's bag, Carl went ahead to the desk and arranged for the room, paying in advance, and then turned and came back to her, and she thought again, seeing his face in the harsh blue light of the lobby, that he looked very ill and tired.

"It's all arranged," he said. "Are you sure you have enough money to last you a couple of days?"

"Yes, thank you. I have plenty."

"Is there anything you need now?"

"I would like some cigarettes."

"Of course. I still don't smoke, you know, so I would never have thought of them."

The way he said it, the way he used the word *still*, it sounded as if he were deliberately recalling old times, trying to get them reestablished on old terms, and she watched him walk over to the tobacco counter for the cigarettes with her intense and oppressive sense of guilt in conflict with her gratitude. The truth was, she had never liked him much even in the old days, even in the good days before the bad days. She had considered him dull and stuffy, possessed even in adolescence of an abortive maturity, and she wondered why she had never suspected his capacity for kindness, that he would be the one, of all she had known, whose compassion would rise in the end above fear and indignation.

He returned with the cigarettes and handed them to her and, taking her arm again, guided her to the elevator. A bellhop had appeared at last and had assumed control of her bag and was waiting with it in the car. At the door, Carl stopped.

"I won't go up with you," he said. "Will you be all right?"

"Yes. Perfectly."

"I'll call you to let you know just when we will leave. It will be soon. Within two or three days, if possible. If I were you, I would stay in the hotel."

"I'll not leave."

"Well—good night, then."

"Good night."

He turned abruptly and walked away through the lobby, and she went up in the elevator and down to her room with the bellhop, and after the bellhop was gone, she sat down and lit one of the cigarettes and began to think again about going back in her mind to a certain time and place, the point of deviance, and though it was probably impossible to isolate it so neatly from all other times and places, since everything is a growth and a result of many causes, there was, nevertheless, the apparent time, the time of understanding, and so she reached it and began to think naturally of Alison.

SECTION 2

Hardly ever, when she remembered, did she go beyond Alison in time, even though Alison was comparatively recent, and this was because Alison was the first beauty and the first trauma and was therefore the beginning of everything that counted later. Even the name had contributed to the sum of factors assuring a certain growth, for the name of Alison was to Lisa altogether beautiful, the kind of name she would have chosen for herself if the choosing had been hers. But she was glad, of course, that the name was not hers after all, but really Alison's, because it is a pleasure, a kind of mild masochism, to have all the beautiful things belong to someone you love and none to yourself.

The truth was, though Lisa had never realized it and still didn't, that Alison was not exceptional at all. At the time she started attending Lisa's school she was sixteen years old, one year older than Lisa herself, and she was a tall, slim girl with brown hair and eyes who was very good at games, especially tennis. Lisa also liked to play tennis, and it was at the courts behind the school that she and Alison met. Lisa was sitting on a bench in the sunlight beside a court, watching a pair of boys finish a set that had gone from deuce to advantage and back to deuce, and she was wishing for someone to come along looking for an opponent, and all of a sudden here was this very attractive girl she had only seen a few times around the school recently, and she was saying hello in the most ordinary sort of way, just exactly as if it were something perfectly routine and not an end and a beginning and something that could never be forgotten.

"My name is Alison Hall," the girl said. "Are you waiting for a game?"

Lisa stood up and smiled and said that she was.

"I'm Lisa Sheridan," she said. "Would you like to play?"

"Are you very good?"

"No. I guess I'm pretty bad, really. I only started playing a few months ago."

"That's all right, then. I'm pretty bad myself."

This was not true, as Lisa soon discovered; it was so great a deviation from the truth, as a matter of fact, that it couldn't be explained or justified as simple modesty or honest self-deprecation. It was Alison's practice to belittle her ability in anything competitive for the dual purpose of minimizing her opponent's accomplishment if she lost and exaggerating her own if she won. This might have been considered a character fault by some, but Lisa would never acknowledge it or think about, it or listen to anyone who suggested it. Not then, that first day she was subjected to it, or ever afterward.

They sat down on the bench together, waiting for the boys to finish their set, and Alison stretched her legs out in front of her and flexed the muscles in them. It was still September, still very warm, and she was wearing white twill shorts that were very brief, like the shorts the boys wore rather than the longer kind worn by most of the girls, and her legs were long and deeply tanned and quite lovely. Lisa considered her own legs much too thin and was secretly rather ashamed of them. Moreover, her skin was very fair and did not tan properly. Now, her eyes following the lines of Alison's flanks and calves, she thought they were the loveliest legs she had ever seen and wished that hers were even half so good. Lifting her eyes, she saw that Alison was watching her with a strange little smile on her lips, and she was certain, all at once, that the other girl was aware of her thoughts and was waiting for her to express them.

She did, though she had not intended to.

"You have lovely legs," she said.

"You think so?"

"Yes. They're very lovely."

"Well, yours are nice too."

"No. You're just saying that. They're much too thin."

"I think they're nice. And you shouldn't be so modest. You're really a pretty girl. I've noticed you before, and I don't mind admitting I've been planning to meet you. Boys always like that pale kind of hair you've got. Almost silver. I'll bet you have plenty of boy friends."

"No, I haven't. I don't know many boys at all. Not well, I mean."

"Why not?"

Actually, Lisa had simply never developed an interest in boys, but she only said, "I don't know. I've never thought about it much."

"Do you ever go out with them?"

"Hardly ever."

"Do you like them?"

"Well, I guess I like them all right."

"I don't. I think boys are the most terrific bores."

She sat on the bench and frowned at the two on the court as if they were the most terrific bores of all. Lisa could not understand her, and she could not understand how it had happened that they were sitting on this bench and talking the way they were, so sort of intimately, when they had only just met. She was not disturbed by it, however, nor in the slightest embarrassed. It was rather exciting, really, not exactly in itself but because it seemed to suggest in a strange way the possibility of excitements that would have to be discovered. What she was most keenly aware of was an intense desire, sudden and consuming, to make a favorable impression, and she regretted, having learned Alison's feeling toward boys, that she had not been more critical herself. She was trying to think of a way to correct her mistake when Alison turned her head and looked at her.

"Girls are much more interesting," Alison said.

"That's right, come to think of it. They are."

"I'd much rather have a girl friend than a boy friend. Wouldn't you?"

Was this a subtle offer of friendship? Lisa's sense of excitement increased even more, and it was extremely pleasant. She had never felt anything quite like it before. She wanted to tell Alison that she would rather have *her* for a friend than any old boy, but it was too soon, after all, and she wasn't prepared to do it. Not yet.

"Girls are more interesting," she said, repeating Alison's dictum.

"Do you have a girl friend?"

"Oh, yes. Several."

"I don't mean like that. I mean a *special* girl friend. Someone you like to be with and to think about and to do all sorts of interesting things with."

Lisa thought about it, and it seemed to her that maybe there were a couple of girls who qualified by Alison's definition, but she had an idea that she thought so only because she did not quite grasp the full significance of Alison's expression, and so she shook her head and replied that she guessed she didn't have any friend exactly like that.

"Do *you*?" she said.

"Not right now. I'm new in town. Didn't you know that?"

"I thought so. I've only seen you around school a few times."

"You mean you really noticed me?"

"Oh, yes."

"Why?"

Alison was now looking at her closely, the little scowl on her face that gave her a kind of dramatic intensity, implying that a great deal more than Lisa supposed might depend upon the answer, and Lisa was suddenly shy and dumb, unable to respond, color creeping up under the clear, pale skin of her face.

"You're blushing," Alison said.

"Am I? I didn't know it."

"Why are you blushing?"

"I don't know."

"Don't you want to tell me why you noticed me?"

"I don't mind."

"Tell me, then."

"Well, because you're so attractive and everything."

"Oh, go on. You're just saying that."

"No, I'm not. It's perfectly true."

The declaration came out much more fiercely than Lisa had intended, and this seemed to please Alison immensely. Her scowl was replaced by a small smile that was at once satisfied and secretive, and she stood up abruptly.

"Those stupid boys are finally finished," she said. "Now we can play tennis."

They went out onto the court and started to play, and it was soon apparent that Lisa was no match. Alison moved swiftly on her strong brown legs, her reflexes functioning with the speed that is essential to excellence in physical games, and there was a masculine power in the flat trajectory of her drives. After four games, Lisa had not won a single point, but Alison did not for this reason relax her game in the slightest. There was a deadly, almost vicious purposeness in the way she scored her points, as if she took a savage pleasure in humiliating her opponent. Strangely enough, though, Lisa did not feel humiliated, or even angry. Ordinarily she was not a particularly good loser and would have quit playing when it became obvious that she had no chance to win. But now she found a pleasure in submitting to her beating that was as strange in its own way as Alison's in giving it to her.

After the final point of the fourth game, more because she was exhausted than because of her inability to score, she left her side of the court and came around the net to Alison.

"You're much too good for me," she said.

"Do you want to quit?"

"Yes. I'm very tired."

"Are you? I'm not. I'm not tired at all."

"You're stronger than I am."

"That's true. I'm really quite strong."

"Besides, I have to be getting home. I enjoyed playing with you, but I'm afraid I didn't give you much opposition."

Alison laughed suddenly, her teeth flashing white in her brown face, and put an arm around Lisa's waist. Lisa could feel the strength in the arm and the heat of Alison's body, was aware intensely of Alison's smooth flank against her own.

"That's all right. I'll teach you."

"Really? I shouldn't think anyone as good as you would want to be bothered."

"Oh, nonsense. The truth is, I like you. I've had a feeling right along that we could be very good friends. Would you like to be friends?"

"Yes."

"Well, that's settled, then. Will you play tennis with me tomorrow afternoon?"

"If you really want me to."

"Of course I want you to. If I didn't, I wouldn't ask. I'm quite sweaty, aren't you?"

"Yes. It's still very hot playing in the sun."

"Do you suppose we could go inside and have a shower?"

"In the school?"

"Of course."

"I don't know about that. I don't think we're supposed to use the showers except after gym classes."

"Oh, come on. What could be the harm in it? You have a locker in the dressing room, don't you?"

"Well, yes. Everyone has a locker."

"I don't. I haven't been assigned one yet. Come on. I'll just share your towel, if you don't mind."

"I ought to be getting home."

"That's all right. I have my father's car. I'll drive you home afterward, and you'll be there just as soon."

The arm around Lisa's waist was imperative, directing her in the way it wanted her to go, and they walked up from the tennis court to a rear entrance to the school and up on the inside to the dressing room on the girls' side of the gymnasium. Miss Mackson, the physical education teacher, was not in the dressing room when they entered, nor was anyone else. Lisa's excitement was out of proportion to the circumstances, but she was also a little uneasy, for she had an idea that there would be trouble if she and Alison were discovered showering after class hours. Her mother and father would be very angry with her if she got into trouble at school, and it would, besides, be very humiliating to have to go before the principal or something. Wishing to get finished and away, she began to undress quickly, sitting on the bench in front of her locker to remove her tennis shoes and socks. Then, standing to complete the undressing, she was conscious all at once of a strange inner conflict, reluctance and eagerness at odds over taking off everything in front of this rather confusing and compelling girl she had only just met and could not quite understand.

Hesitating, she looked at Alison and saw that the other girl was already naked and was watching her with the small smile on her lips that seemed to be the emotional antithesis of the intent smile that expressed her dislike. Stripped, its smooth brown broken in two places by bands of white the sun had not reached, Alison's body had a hard clean look of grace that even her thin shirt and brief shorts had not completely shown, her hips assuming in nakedness a boyish narrowness, her shoulders an added breadth."What's the matter?" she said.

"Nothing."

"What are you waiting for?"

"I'm not waiting for anything. I'll be ready in just a minute."

She finished undressing in a hurry, and they went back to the shower stalls and stood for quite a while under the hot water and for a few seconds under the cold, and then Alison shut off the water and turned to Lisa, and it was perfectly plain all of a sudden that they had come to the time for some kind of decision, but afterward, when Lisa thought back to it, there didn't really seem to have been any decision or choice at all, but only something that had to begin and did. At first, for some time after the first time, there was a fear that sometimes assumed the dimensions of terror, and there was a feeling of guilt that was based less on a conviction of transgression than on the certainty that her mother and father and brother and practically everyone else would consider it so. But against the burden of fear and guilt, which gradually lightened, there was the compensation of Alison and Alison's special friendship. They were together almost all the time, and spent nights at each other's house and all things like that, and everyone thought how inseparable they were and that it was really quite sweet and charming; and everything was fine, except for the sickness of fear and guilt, all through the fall and the winter and right up into the spring, which was the time Miss Mackson found the note.

Lisa had written the note to Alison and was going to pass it to her when she got the chance, and this was nothing new or different, because she wrote a note every once in a while to tell Alison again how wonderful it was to be her friend and just how she felt about everything, but perhaps it was foolish to put it down on paper that way when you couldn't possibly expect anyone else to understand about it if it became known. It wasn't really necessary to write the notes, of course, because all that was in them could have been spoken, but somehow it seemed easier to find just the right words for it when there was time to select them carefully and write them down. Anyhow, the note was written, and it was in her jacket pocket when she went in to gym, and later, when she came out, it was gone. She was very frightened and went back to the dressing room to look for it, but it wasn't there. After that she didn't know what to do, and though she didn't know it yet, there was nothing to be done at all, because Miss Mackson had found it.

What followed was something she tried afterward to repress, and she had no clear recollection of it, the natural sequence of events, but of only an incoherent kaleidoscope of ugly and terrifying scenes. She found herself trapped inside a hard perimeter of danger, a circle of cold faces set in lines of revulsion—her father's, her mother's, her brother Carl's. Beyond them, in the darkness beyond the perimeter, were all the vicariously aggrieved and violated, and she knew for the first time in her life the loneliness and terror of the one who was different in a way that was unacceptable, the person apart. Her isolation, for a while, was actually physical. In her room, quarantined, she watched from her window the assumption of spring by earth, the progress of green growth and the early rain and the assaults of gusty wind, and she thought of Alison and wanted Alison and wondered when, if ever, she would see Alison again.

In time, of course, she was restored to the forms of normalcy, to the associations and relative freedom of school, but she was now disturbed and uncertain in relationships she had formerly sustained with ease, and though she was aware that the secret of her transgression was guarded by a few, she could not lose her sense of separation, of acceptance irrevocably repudiated, and she felt rejection in every contact. This feeling did not begin and end at the door of her home. She felt it most of all in her own family, in inverse ratio to their stiff efforts to conceal it, and after a while she actually began to pity them in their confusion and shock, their utter inability to understand or accept what had happened. Not so much to her, really, as to them. The terrible threat to their respectability.

She saw Alison, and there was nothing altered, in spite of disaster and disgrace, in the way she felt about the other girl, or in the degree of her longing. She wanted to speak to her and to touch her and to receive the assuring commitment of the small smile, but this was now impossible. She wondered if Alison had suffered and was unhappy and above all if she was angry because of the note. She could not bear the thought of Alison's being angry. Of the multitude of threats in the strange and transformed world, this was the one that caused her, when she considered it, the greatest despair. Looking to Alison for reassurance, for the slightest sign in passing, she received nothing, no smile, no gesture, no word dropped softly. The truth was, Alison seemed entirely unaware of her, as if there had never been between them a discovery or a dedication or any feeling whatever.

The year aged and spring passed and school closed, and after the closing of school, with even the brief sight of Alison in passing now denied her, Lisa could bear the separation no longer. She began to walk by herself, when she could get away, along the streets near Alison's home, and once she saw the other girl with her father, and several times with her mother, and at last, as she had been hoping, alone. They were on opposite sides of the street at the time, and Lisa, crossing over, felt in the space of the crossing a mounting and hurting happiness that reduced to insignificance all that had happened because of Alison or might ever happen because of her later. "Alison," she said.

Alison stopped and turned. It was not the small smile she displayed, however, but the antithetic scowl. "What do you want?-"

"I just want to talk with you, Alison. I've been so lonely for you."

"Have you? Well, you'd better get used to it, I guess, because you'll be lonely for me for a long time as far as I'm concerned."

"Haven't you missed me? Aren't you glad to see me?"

"No. I wish I wasn't seeing you now, and I hope I never see you again."

"Why? Why, Alison?"

"Because you're a fool, that's why."

"Because of the note?"

"Yes, because of the note. Only a fool would have been so careless."

"I'm sorry. I admit it was careless."

"Well, I should think sol You damn near ruined me."

"I said I was sorry, Alison. Please don't be angry."

"Of course I'm angry. Do you understand what I've been through? Do you think I like being looked at as if I were filthy or something? Do you think I enjoy being watched all the time and hardly ever allowed to go anywhere alone? If I were even seen talking with you, I'd be in trouble all over again."

"Does it matter so much? It doesn't to me. I'd be in trouble too, but it doesn't matter at all if only you won't be angry and we can be friends again."

"Are you crazy? It's impossible."

"Please, Alison. It's all been so terrible, and no one understands anything about it. How it really was, I mean. I'll kill myself if you won't be friends."

"Oh, don't be so stupid."

"I will. I swear I will."

"Well, go ahead and kill yourself, then. I'm sure I'd be better off if you did."

"Don't talk like that. Please don't."

In the urgency of her supplication, Lisa moved forward and lifted a hand, and Alison backed away. Lisa's intensity frightened her a little, and she wondered uneasily if the crazy little fool were actually capable of killing herself after all. She hadn't really thought so, and that's why she had spoken so brutally, but she wouldn't actually want anything like that to happen, because she would surely be implicated herself, under the circumstances, and would have to suffer for it one way or another.

"Don't touch me," she said.

"I won't hurt you, Alison. I only want you to be kind to me again."

"Go away."

"Please, Alison."

"Go away, I tell you. If you don't go away and leave me alone, I'll tell my father that you molested me. Then you'll really be in trouble."

Turning abruptly, Alison walked back the way she hid come, the long legs that had been strong and brown in the late summer sun carrying her away swiftly. For a moment Lisa was on the point of running after her, but the desperate moment passed and was gone, the moment and Alison gone together and for good, and she stood there fixed and trembling, the incredibly beautiful name dying in her throat with an ugly strangled sound.

So it ended. So it died on a sidewalk with a whimper. Lisa carried the corpse of it home inside her and sat over it in her room. She considered dying herself, how it might best be done, but what she wanted was merely to die and not to kill herself, which are different things, and so she continued to live and entered a long armistice, precariously balanced between this way to go and that way, the way before Alison and the way Alison had shown her, and it could have been in that time, depending upon circumstances, either of the ways.

Then there was one summer, a short while one summer, when she was at a certain lake resort on vacation with her family, and there was a girl there she had come to know, and something had started and grown between them and had eventually ended in the way things end that are a part of a summer and are not expected to survive it. Afterward it had not been thought of much or remembered long, except as an infrequent associate of some subsequent incident, and even yet, even after the second overt time, there was still the other way available, though it had become, because of the summer at the lake, just so much less likely.

Depression became an uncontrollable factor in her life. Whereas it had previously come infrequently with a discernible logic, the specific result of causes that could be isolated and examined, it now came without apparent reason, just came and remained for longer and longer periods, was often just there waiting for her when she awoke in the morning, or came to her in the middle of the night, or while she was going about her affairs in the course of the day. Because of this, she deliberately took an overdose of barbiturates when she was twenty-one, but she did not die and was sent by her frightened parents to a psychiatrist who learned a great deal about her but did very little for her. This happened in her third year in Midland City College, and in her fourth and last year there was an associate professor in the Department of Foreign Languages. The associate professor was a young woman named Jeanne Marot who spoke with a French accent and had actually been born and educated in France. She was quite attractive in a sleek, angular way, like a clothes model in an expensive fashion magazine, and she was, besides, as it developed, quite aggressive when she was reasonably certain of the response to her aggression, and it seemed for a while that she was the answer to everything, but of course she was not. This was perfectly apparent after a few months, and, anyhow, the affair had become by then extremely precarious and threatening.

The summer after the last year in college was the worst in her life, a period of chronic melancholia that made the performance of the simplest act, a monstrous burden and a terrifying threat, as if any change in condition at all might destroy her precarious balance and place her in incomprehensible peril, and when she thought back to the summer afterward she could never understand how she survived it and sometimes wished that she hadn't. Because the summer was so bad, because it was necessary to survival to do something, almost anything, it was quite simple in the end to make the decision about Bella. They met in a park where Lisa had gone because home had long since become intolerable and because the park was simply a place to go that was not home, and their common denominator was something not difficult to establish by simple techniques of approach and response. They met the next day in the same place, seemingly by accident, and the next day after that openly by appointment; and a week later Lisa moved into the apartment on the south side of the city, and Bella was someone to adhere to, an object to give allegiance, the symbol to Lisa of what she considered a definitive decision. She left home after an icy scene with her family in which horror was disguised as anger and everything was understood but not mentioned.

* * * *

And now, in a strange room in a strange hotel, she realized that the deviate way was a way that had cured no ill and established no peace, and that she would have to return after all to the other way, the way she had thought rejected forever, and she would not return because she wanted to do so for any reason that was essential to her real needs and hungers, but simply because she did not possess whatever qualities were necessary to survival among the perils and oppressions of aberrance.

Rising from the chair, she went to a window and looked out and saw that neither the snow nor the wind had diminished. And at that moment in Corinth, three hundred miles away, Emerson and Ed Page were lying asleep in their bed, each in the arms of the other; and Avery Lawes, in the brick house on High Street, was also lying in bed but was not asleep and in no one's arms.

CHAPTER III

SECTION 1

There was a terrace in the sun, and a swimming pool below the terrace, and beyond the swimming pool, sand and the ocean. Around the pool and on the sand and sometimes in the ocean there were brown men and brown women who were not quite naked, and after a while, after the passing of hours and days, he was able to look at them with practically no feeling of any kind. He sat on the terrace in a bright canvas sling, which was really half sitting and half lying, and the white light was softened by the thin filters of his closed lids to red that sometimes deepened to black, and in the soft red-and-black world behind his lids were a beautiful golden woman who had been dead a long time and a frozen gray man who had been dead a short time; and it was necessary to see them now, if he was to see them ever, without perversion or distortion and in true relationship to himself.

This is how it was, he thought. This was the beginning of awareness, and it was night, and I lay in my room in the house on High Street, and because I was very young I was supposed to be asleep, but I wasn't. Lying in my bed, I could look out to the east and see the moonlight on the crest of the ridge beyond the river, but I couldn't see the river itself because it was hidden at the foot of the bluff that dropped away at the lower end of the back yard, and I thought about the river, how it would look silver in the moonlight, and pretty soon I heard a car come up the drive from the street and stop in the portico, and I knew it was my father and mother coming back from wherever they'd been, and I thought it was pretty early for it. I quit looking at the crest of the ridge and thinking about the river and started waiting for the sounds of the door opening and closing in the lower hall, and the heavy steps and the light steps coming up the stairs, and the heavy voice and the light voice talking and laughing and passing in the upper hall, all very softly and subdued because of me, because it was supposed that I was sleeping. This night, though, as I lay and listened, the door opened and closed as usual, and the steps came and passed as usual, but there was no sound of voices, no restrained talking and laughing, and this was not usual and not at all right.

The acoustics of night are very strange. At night you can hear many things that are not heard in the day, the creaks and whispers and sighs of sound, and you can hear voices in a room with a thick wall between. You cannot hear precisely what is said, the significant arrangement of vowels and consonants, but you can hear their inflections and determine their temper and know by their quality if they are spoken in love or amity or anger. As I heard and knew, lying and listening in my room to the hard voices in the room of my parents.

They were very angry, my father's with a quality of measured fury, my mother's with a kind of icy and studied contempt. I had never heard them speak like that to each other, or to anyone else, and it made me afraid of the night and the familiar things that the night made unfamiliar, and I wished that I had gone to sleep as I was supposed to and had not heard them come in and begin talking behind their closed door. I tried to quit listening, to ignore the disturbing flow of sound from the other room, and I looked out again at this moonlit crest and tried to picture again the moonlit river that could not be seen, but the angry voices could not be rejected, and now it was my father who was doing most of the talking, and his voice had risen, and this was exceedingly strange and frightening, because he was a man who ordinarily said very little and said that softly. I had never consciously acknowledged a preference for either of my parents, but now I began to have a feeling of resentment toward my father and of alliance with my mother, because she was gay and golden and beautiful beyond description, and if there was something wrong between them, it was surely my father's fault. I thought that it was not right for him to talk to her that way, with his voice rising on a cadence of fury, and then I began to think that he would certainly stop if I were to go down and open their door, because it was an accepted rule among all people who amounted to anything that parents should not make scenes before their children, and so I got out of bed and went out into the hall on my bare feet and down to the door of their room.

I put a hand on the knob of the door and stood there with the fear in me suddenly rising, afraid of the consequences of intruding on two people who were all at once strangers, and after a silence, his voice resuming its deadly modulation, my father said, "I think that I should kill you, and perhaps I shall," and my mother laughed and said, "You won't kill me, and you won't even divorce me, and you will do nothing at all, in fact, because anything you might do would cause a scandal, and it is unthinkable that there should ever be a scandal in the family of Lawes, which is the first family in Corinth, which is God's chosen town." Then I turned the knob and the door swung into the room away from me.

My mother was sitting at her dressing table with her back to me, and she was holding a brush behind her head as if she had just finished a stroke down the length of her shining hair, and I could picture her sitting there brushing her hair all the time my father was saying all those angry things to her and answering him back with the cold contempt in her voice, and I had to admit in justice to him that it was something that would probably make anyone furious. I could see the reflection of her face in the mirror, and she could see me in the mirror too, and her eyes widened and she slowly laid the brush or, the glass top of the dressing table and reached up automatically with the other hand to clutch the top of her robe. She turned on the bench to look at me directly, and my father turned also in his position between us, and the two of them looked at me together.

Finally my mother said in a normal voice, "What are you doing up, darling? I thought you were asleep hours ago?"

"I tried to sleep, but I couldn't," I said. "I was watching out the window, how the moonlight was and everything."

"That's very nice, but perhaps you could have gone to sleep if you had closed your eyes and tried a little harder. Did we disturb you when we came in?"

"You didn't exactly disturb me, but I could hear you talking."

"Why did you get up? Are you frightened?"

"You sounded angry. I thought maybe you would stop being angry if I came down and opened the door."

My father came over and put a hand on my head. "We were talking about something that caused us to lose our tempers with each other. That was pretty foolish, wasn't it?"

"Why did you say you might kill Mother?"

"Did I say that? I certainly didn't mean it. It shows you how foolish it is to become angry."

"Why did Mother say you wouldn't divorce her? Did you say you would do it?"

"Your mother said things she didn't mean, just as I did. You mustn't think about it any more or let it bother you in the least. Now you had better go back to bed."

"I would like for Mother to come with me."

"Is that necessary?"

My mother stood up and walked over to us. I could see the shadow of her body under her thin robe, and she was wearing a scent that I have never forgotten and can still smell, even at this moment, though I have not wanted to remember it, and she put an arm around my shoulders and said, "Of course I will come with you. Come along, darling."

We went to my room together, and I got into bed again, and she sat on the edge of the bed beside me, and it was then still a great pleasure to look at her and touch her and smell the scent of her.

"It's lovely," she said. "The moonlight on the ridge, I mean. I can understand why you stayed awake to look at it."

"I didn't stay awake on purpose," I said. "It just happened."

She sat there looking out the window with a soft light on her face that seemed like it was coming through from the inside, and I lay there thinking that it was more beautiful by far than the moonlight on the ridge, or even on the river, and after a while I went to sleep, and she went away.

That was the beginning of awareness, but not yet of knowing, and my mother and father lived in a cold compromise that lasted for months, and whatever was wrong between them that night went right on being wrong, and it looked like it was going on forever, and then it changed. Something happened, and I don't know what it was, but there was certainly something, because they were gay with each other again, and went out together at night, and came home talking and laughing, and slept in the same room and all that. It was late in the summer of that year that we went to Mexico City, and I remember Chapultepec Park as clearly as if it were yesterday but nothing else, and everything was fine until the Mexican musician. (Oh, God, that reminds me of the other night in Em Page's bar, and at home later, and what a thundering, bloody bore I must have made of myself! I must send Em a card and apologize, but I suppose he hopes devoutly that I never enter his place again, and I can't blame him if he does.)

I didn't know at the time that it was because of the Mexican that we came home so soon, of course, and didn't know it until years later, after my mother was dead and my father told me about that and other things so that I would understand why everything in our life had gone sour, but I knew that it was because of something bad, something wrong between them again, and by the time my father finally got around to telling me I already knew how my mother had been, that she liked to sleep around, and a lousy Mexican musician more or less didn't make a hell of a lot of difference one way or another.

The cold compromise, following Mexico City, was resumed and was complete and was never afterward violated, and the compromise seemed to be that they would maintain the appearance of marriage without the substance, and for a long time, because I was very young and knew nothing, I was sure that my mother was good and right for no other reason than that she was incredibly beautiful, and that the wrong between them, whatever it was, was his. Later, after the day I saw her with the man who cut the grass and took care of the flowers, I assumed the other extreme and thought that that fault was all hers, and I hated her and was sickened by her and could not stand her near me. My revulsion was something I could neither hide nor explain, and it is possible that it contributed to the sum of factors that caused her to kill herself, and if it did, I'm sorry, but I couldn't help it. Now, looking back, I can see that it was either the fault of both or the fault of neither, and I believe really that the latter is true, that she could no more help what was in her blood or brain or glands, or wherever it was, than he could help the peculiar social cowardice that made it easier to suffer a life-long private degradation rather than to suffer even briefly a public one. The creed of the Laweses, the God-damn cowardly creed of the Laweses, and I suppose that I am as faithful a subscriber to it as any of the others before me, and as great a coward.

This man who cut the grass and took care of the flowers. I can't even remember his name, and this is probably one of the things that I've repressed and deliberately refused to remember. But I can still see him quite clearly in my mind as he was when he worked for us, his tall strong body burned brown by the sun, his white teeth flashing in his dark face with a bold arrogance that seemed to remind you that he might be only a kind of handyman in the yard and gardens, but that he had his own points of superiority if you cared to notice. He worked for us in the spring and summer and early autumn of two years, and it was in the summer of the second year that I saw my mother with him in the arbor by the bluff above the river, and it is now time to think about it clearly, long past time. Here in this warm sunshine, on this bright terrace, it is time to bring it out of the dark into the light and to see it for what it was and nothing more, illicit and wanton and a breach of fidelity but basically normal just the same, nothing at all to sicken a life for more than two decades.

There was this garden swing in the deep back yard, and I liked to sit there in the summer and look down into the bottoms at the gray ribbon of river that had come a thousand miles to this place, and beyond the river was the rich bottom land running east to the ridge. I liked to sit there in the swing and look at the ridge and river and think about how it must have been when there were Indians here, and Conestoga wagons cross-ing the river on rafts on the way west, and my father said that this hadn't actually been so long ago, but it seemed to me that it surely must have been ages and that he only thought otherwise because he was himself so old. At that time he must have been all of forty, give a year or two either way, but there was already in him a chill grayness that made him seem much more.

It was this hot summer afternoon, one of these summer afternoons when all time and motion seem suspended and there is the softest, sleepiest kind of drone in the air that must come from thousands of small things that can't be located, and I thought it would be pleasant to sit in the garden swing by the bluff, and I went down there. I sat in the swing and felt very drowsy, and after a while I was conscious of the sounds from the arbor over to my right, and the sounds seemed to be a kind of rustling and heavy breathing. I listened and looked over at the little house, which had lattice walls with very narrow cracks that you couldn't see through from a distance, and after a minute or two I got up and went over close enough to see inside, and there they were on the floor. I wanted to move, but I couldn't, and I stood there until it was all over, and then I turned and walked away very quietly, and I have thought later that that must be the way the world will end, not in noise and fire and physical pain, but with everything disintegrating in an instant in utter silence.

And now, remembering deliberately after all this time, I am still sick and not cured. I am sick with the thought of gasping passion and the cruel hunger. Catharsis futile.

She was sick too, of course, in her own way, and in the end she found her own cure. One balm for many fevers; who wrote that? Someone wrote it, and the balm of death, and it was the balm and the cure she found. It should have been anticipated; it was forecast in the quality of her personality in her last years, which should have been among her early years, in the intensity of an overt gayety possessing the shading of despair and in the fierce activity that was like the product of delirium And I have wondered if my father did not actually expect it and look forward to it and consciously do nothing to prevent it. However that may have been; she came home one night and went into her room and took something and lay down to die. She was dead in the morning, and my father found her there and locked the door and went downstairs to call the doctor. The doctor came, and he was a friend of the family, of course, and it was all hushed up, the way she had done it, just as unpleasant things were always hushed up when they happened to a Lawes. I didn't see her myself until the funeral, when the warm, hungry flesh was bloodless and cold, and we buried her; and in the cemetery my father stood at the edge of her grave with no grief or relief or regret apparent in his face, as if nothing had ever begun or ended.

So she is dead, and my father is dead, but I am not. That's the point. That is what it comes to. I am not dead and do not want to die. Not wanting to die, I must therefore arrange to live. It's that simple. It is really very simple indeed. One must think it through logically, that's all. It is quite clear, for instance, that I am sick and dying, though I wish to live, and that my sickness is abhorrence and rejection of women in the basic function of woman, and that this abhorrence and rejection has become, through a kind of psychic diffusion or something, an abhorrence and rejection of life itself. It follows that I must cure the one in order to cure the other. To reduce it to simplest terms, I must learn to love. Surely this is something that can be done.

How warm the sun is. How softly it touches the body. It seems a long time from the gray days that get inside you and become part of you. It seems a long, long way from the cold and snow of Corinth. Was it only Saturday that I was there? Was it only a few days' ago that Em Page drove me home with a load of Scotch? Oh, Christ, what a fool I made of myself! I wonder what in hell Em must think of me? I must remember to get that card off...

SECTION 2

The room's ocean side was all glass. Accommodations at the hotel, she thought, even though it was not one of the extremely expensive places, were surely costing Carl quite a lot, and she considered it additional evidence of the remarkable depths of kindness and generosity in him that she had never suspected before. She stood in front of the wall of glass with her back to the room and looked out over terrace and sand and not-quite-naked bodies to the glittering blue water spreading out to the remote blue sky. She was very tired from her trip, and her bath had not refreshed her as she had hoped, and what she really wanted and needed was a very strong drink. Her eyes followed the line of junction of sky anti water, and she was not particularly depressed at that moment, in spite of the tiredness, but she wished that Carl would come for her and take her down to the bar.

As if in answer to the wish, he knocked on the door. She knew that it was he, because there was no one else who could possibly have a reason for knocking, and so she turned and called across the room to him to enter. He came in and stopped and looked around and rubbed his hands together like a man coming upon something suddenly and finding it unexpectedly pleasing.

"Very nice," he said. "Are you comfortable?"

"Comfortable is hardly the word for it. The room must be quite expensive."

"Oh, nonsense. I can afford it, you know. You're looking lovely, Lisa."

"Do you think so? Thank you very much."

She was, as a matter of fact. After her bath, she had put on a thin black sheath dress that gave rather startling; emphasis to her pale skin and hair.

With her small breasts and narrow hips, she looked much younger than she actually was, possessing an almost adolescent; charm.

"You look about sixteen," he said.

"No, Carl, really. Don't exaggerate so."

"Well, a slight exaggeration, maybe. But only slight. You never showed your age, Lisa. I remember that you always looked much younger than you were. I came to see if you would care to go down for a drink."

"Yes. I was just wishing that you would come and ask for me."

"That's good, then. Do you suppose I will have trouble getting you into the bar?"

"Why should you?"

"Because of your age, I mean. No minors allowed."

It was a joke and he laughed at it, his tired and ill-looking face creasing and opening around a soft expulsion of air. He was obviously determined to resume an earlier relationship, to proceed from this point in the pretense that it had never been interrupted, that there had been on her part no betrayal, no desertion, no aberrance. She had again for a moment the feeling inside her of dry and silent weeping, all that apparently was left to her of the relief of tears, and she laughed with him at his joke, feeling no laughter at all within.

"I'll carry my birth certificate," she said, and they went downstairs feeling quite at ease with one another, for the first time as if they were really beginning a holiday. The bar was not large and was crowded with patrons and humming with the subdued confusion of conversations against a background of muted music, but they found a table in a corner and sat down, and after a while a waiter came and stood beside the table.

"What would you like?" Carl said.

"A daiquiri, I think."

"Frozen?"

"No, not frozen."

"Good. I could never see the sense in a frozen daiquiri." He looked up at the waiter. "Two daiquiris," he said.

The waiter went away and returned pretty soon with the daiquiris. They were cold and tart and very good. Lisa drank some of hers and felt the rum begin to work. "When would you like to have dinner?" Carl asked.

"I don't know." She listened for a moment to the voices and the music. "Not for quite a while, really. I'm not at all hungry."

"Do you want to eat here or somewhere else? Perhaps we should ask about the good places."

"I'd just as soon eat here. It's very nice here."

"It is, isn't it? It was recommended to me by a fellow in Midland City who was down a year ago. I should have come myself much sooner. Long ago."

He sounded reflective and wistful, as if he were reviewing the lost chances of his life. He was thinking, probably, that he had had very little fun out of living. And he looked as if he hadn't, his face appearing older than it was, even in the soft and flattering light of the bar, thin skin gray and dry and loose on its bone structure. He had never at home, Lisa remembered, reacted to anything at all with excitement or sign of genuine pleasure, and she felt now that she had somehow contributed to this inadequacy, this effect of flatness, and she was suddenly oppressed by her recurrent conviction of guilt. For a moment she was absolutely certain that she should never have come here with him, that it would never work for good but only for disaster; and that she was not only peculiarly vulnerable herself to corruption and misery but was also a kind of carrier of these things, a source of contagion for everyone who had anything to do with her. She thought that it would be a kindness to him if she were to get up without a word and walk away and never again see him or speak to him or have any contact with him of any kind, and the compulsion was very strong to act upon the thought, but she merely lifted her glass instead and looked at him over the edge.

His attention had been diverted, and he was staring intently at someone who had come in and got onto a stool at the bar. Following the direction of his gaze, she saw a slim back in a white jacket and, beyond in the glass, a blur of features in a narrow frame.

"That fellow there," he said. "I'd swear that I know him."

"Maybe he's someone from Midland City."

"No. I don't think so. If he were from home, I'd remember. I have quite a good memory for names and faces. Well, never mind. Probably he only resembles someone I know. Are you ready for another daiquiri?"

"Yes, please."

He signaled a waiter. The waiter came and picked up their glasses and carried them away. The muted, canned music went on and on. King Cole singing something. Later there would be a live entertainer, a young woman who played the piano and sang unusual songs that you couldn't hear just anywhere, but now it was King Cole canned. The waiter brought the fresh drinks and Lisa drank some. She was losing her feeling of guilt again, her compulsion to run. Here was the world with her in it, and things were this way or that way, and there was no need to torture yourself about them.

"Avery Lawes," Carl said.

"What?"

"His name is Avery Lawes."

"The man at the bar?"

"Yes. I knew him in college. Classmates. I suppose it's been eight, nine years since I've seen him."

"Really? It's remarkable that you should recognize him so quickly."

"Well, I have a good memory for names and faces. But I said that, didn't I? He lives in Corinth. Used to, anyhow. Corinth is a town across state from home. Not a large place. About thirty thousand, I think."

"I know."

"It's a nice town. Prosperous. Lots of money in Corinth. Some good families there too. I guess the Lawes family was about the most prominent of them all. Still is, I suppose. Money and background. There was a Lawes served a term as governor about twenty years ago. Avery's grandfather, I think."

"To hounds, to hunt, and away."

"What?"

"Never mind. I was just making a joke."

"Oh."

He stared at her blankly, obviously trying to see the humor of it, in what way it was a joke, and she was ashamed of the impulse that had made her say it, her irritation; and she reminded herself again of his enormous kindness and generosity and, above all, of his sincere efforts to understand her and reclaim her. She did not deserve such consideration and was not at all sure that she could respond to it, or at least sustain her response indefinitely to it, or even for any considerable length of time.

"It wasn't funny," she said.

"Well, perhaps I'm a little dull. Never was able to appreciate irony and things like that." He lifted his glass and took a small swallow and set the glass down again. "I'd rather like to speak to Lawes. Do you mind if I do?"

"Not at all. Do as you like about it."

"Excuse me, then?"

"Of course."

He got up and walked toward the bar, and she picked up her daiquiri and drank it quickly and signaled the waiter to bring her another. She would have to be careful about her drinking, she thought. She had quite a capacity for it and did not get drunk easily—not sloppy, out-of-control drunk, anyhow—but there was the very important matter of mood to consider. If she drank too little, the alcohol acted only as a kind of irritant, and she was likely to become nasty and say things she would afterward be sorry for; and if she drank too much she became terribly depressed and started thinking about everything that had happened to her and that it would be much better for her and everyone else if she were dead. And so drinking became in the first place the delicate operation of taking just enough to get the proper lift, the rather lilting feeling of compatibility with herself, and in the second place the even more delicate operation of taking just enough thereafter to sustain the feeling, which was a very difficult thing to do and required lots of practice.

The third drink arrived, and she tasted it, approaching now the delicate point of sustenance. With a pleasant sense of detachment, she watched the action at the bar, the pattern of diffident action and reaction occurring when one person undertakes to renew with another an acquaintance that had been interrupted long ago and had been no more than casual in the beginning. She could not hear what was said, of course, but she could have supplied almost literally the words to go with the observable expressions and gestures and hesitations. "Excuse me, old man. Aren't you Avery Lawes?"

"Yes," lifting his head and twisting on the stool, "yes, I am."

"Sheridan. Carl Sheridan. I'm afraid you don't remember me."

"No. No. Sorry."

"The University. Old what's-his-name's class in Investments. Remember? We graduated together."

"Oh, yes. My God, yes. Sheridan. Carl Sheridan. Inexcusable of me not to have remembered immediately. Well, it's been a long time."

"Certainly has. How have you been, old man?"

"Fine, fine. Working and getting older."

"Still living in Corinth?"

"Yes. No place on earth to live but Corinth, you know. Family's been there for eons."

"I've been right in Midland City myself. Hardly ever get away. Just down here now to recuperate from a spot of pneumonia. Doctor said I ought to come. Takes something like that, I guess, to jar a man loose."

"Yes. Seems like it. Will you have a drink?"

"No, thanks. I'd like to, but I have one waiting for me at the table over there. Have my sister with me."

"Sister? Not married yet, then, I take it."

"No. Never had the time for it. That's my story, anyhow. Truth is, women don't like me."

Laughter. Polite laughter for the little joke.

"Glad to hear it. It's a relief to learn that I'm not the only bachelor left of the old crowd."

"Really? Not married yourself? I should have bet you'd take the plunge long ago."

"Not I. Hopelessly inveterate, I'm afraid."

"Are you expecting someone?"

"To meet me here? No. I'm strictly on my own."

"In that case, why don't you have a drink with my sister and me at our table?"

"Oh, I don't want to intrude."

"Nonsense, old man. We'd love to have you. If you really aren't committed, I'm going to insist."

"Well, if you're sure it won't be an intrusion."

"Quite the contrary. Be a genuine pleasure. You know how it is between a brother and sister. All right for a while, but eventually it gets pretty dull. Especially for the sister. Come along, old man. Just bring your glass with you."

Now Avery Lawes stood up, glass in hand, and came with Carl across the room to the table, and Lisa, watching them come, could see that Lawes was a slim, erect man with a graceful carriage and a rather narrow, good-looking face. His nose was finely shaped, and there was about his mouth a softness and sensitivity that indicated not so much weakness as vulnerability. Lisa noticed these things objectively, with no emotional accompaniment except that of a vague reluctance to emerge from her semi-isolation and engage in a routine of sociability with a man she didn't know and didn't want to know. "My sister Lisa," Carl said. "Lisa, this is Avery Lawes." Lisa smiled and held out a hand, and he took it briefly and released it. His fingers were dry and hard, with very little flesh on the bones, and the touch of them was not offensive. He bent forward slightly from the hips. "How do you do, Miss Sheridan," he said.

She said that she was doing fine. "Won't you sit down?" she said.

He took a chair across from her. He drank from his glass, and she saw that it was Scotch he was drinking. On the rocks. It followed, she thought. First family of Corinth and all that. High class stuff. Why did high class stuff almost always drink high class Scotch?

"Carl tells me you were in the University together," she said. She laughed. "You can see that we were talking about you."

"Convinced I knew you the moment you came in," Carl said. "Just took me a minute or two to place you."

"It's remarkable that you remembered me at all. After so long a time."

"I have a good memory for names and faces." Realizing that he had said this twice before, Carl shot an almost ludicrously contrite look at Lisa. "I mean, it's just one of those little knacks a person has sometimes. Would you like to have that drink freshened?"

"It's Scotch. I'll finish it and have another."

He finished it. Carl finished his daiquiri. Lisa, nursing her third for sustenance, said in response to Carl's inquiry that she was not ready yet. The waiter came and left and came back, and everyone was beginning to feel pretty good, not drunk but just temporarily dissociated from the three people they would recover later in the night or wake up with in the morning.

"That class in Investments," Carl said. "The professor's name. I've been trying to remember it. It was Barnsdorf."

"That's it. Barnsdorf. It was Barnsdorf, all right."

"I kept thinking Barnswell and Barnstorm. It was Barnsdorf, though. Wacky old boy. There was a fellow at the frat house who did a perfect imitation of him."

"Yes. Nutty as a peach orchard bore, they used to call him. I never knew why a peach orchard bore was considered particularly nutty, but that's what they called him. Not so nutty at that, though, I guess. I understand he made over a million dollars just playing the market."

"I've heard that myself, but I never quite believed it."

"You never can tell about these odd old boys. Supposed to be all theory and no common sense, but sometimes they're pretty shrewd. Sometimes they surprise you. Wonder if old Barnsdorf is still living?"

"Oh, I should think so. Been some publicity if he'd died. Especially if he'd left over a million dollars."

"That's right, isn't it? That's a way to tell if he really has it. All we have to do is wait for him to die." Avery turned to Lisa. "Is this your first time in Miami?"

"Yes. We only arrived today."

"Is that so? Only been here four days myself. Are you staying long?"

"I don't know, really. Carl has been ill. He came down to rest and get some sunshine."

"So he told me. Hope you didn't come along for the same reason. Have you been ill too?"

She felt all at once a strong and dangerous compulsion to tell him. Yes, she wanted to say, I have been ill too, I have been ill for many years with an illness that is a result of learning something wrong at a time when it should have been learned right, or perhaps of not learning at all something which should have been learned naturally in the normal process of ceasing to be one phase of person and beginning to be another, and still again, perhaps it is something you are born with and can't help, and the simple truth is that no one actually seems to know what causes it, or what to do about it, least of all the person who has it. You were talking about the old professor at the University, Mr. Lawes. You said he was odd. That is the name of my illness, Mr. Lawes. I suffer from the illness of oddness. For instance, would you believe it, I can look at you and talk with you and ever touch you without revulsion, but I cannot possibly understand how any woman on earth could get excited about the prospect of sharing your life or your bed, even in return for the privilege of becoming a Lawes of Corinth. On the other hand, I can remember a girl named Alison from a long time back, and a woman named Bella from a very short time back, and I can remember others in between these two, and for these I had, and have now in remembrance, a feeling that would astonish you. Isn't this odd of me? Isn't this very odd? There is a name for this oddness, Mr. Lawes, and the name derives from the name of an island where a woman named Sappho once lived and wrote poetry and was, they say, very beautiful. It is a name for those with this illness of oddness, the illness that I have, and it is not pleasant to be odd in a way that is different from the oddnesses that are accepted, like that of the old man who was only good for laughs and possibly a million dollars. If you are odd in a way that is not accepted, you are quite likely to suffer for it. Do you understand me? It is this conflict, this threat of massive retaliation, that is never lost entirely from the consciousness, even if it is never executed, that nourishes a sickness of guilt and diffuse fear and in the end quite possibly destroys you. So I have been ill too, and I am still ill, and I have come to Miami to sit in the sun. My brother has brought me here, and I know very well what he is thinking. Would you like to know? He is thinking with great innocence that a husband would cure me. He is thinking that if I deliberately adopted the form of normalcy the substance of normalcy would develop in its own time. He is thinking that I am really a very pretty woman with a good background and that it is his duty to guide me to an eligible man and to encourage my cultivation of this man. Object, matrimony. A kind of desperate asylum, if you follow me. And do you know something? Being aware of this, I am inclined to submit. Rather, let us say, I have been driven to submit. Not because I am convinced that it is the cure he thinks, but because I am convinced that there is at least no other. And I will tell you something else. Though he wouldn't admit it and probably doesn't even realize it, Carl is at this moment thinking of you, and I am thinking myself that you are, of all the men I've known or am likely to know, quite possibly the least offensive. Do you hear that? Do you understand me?

Better run, Mr. Lawes. Better get up at once and run as if the devil were after you, for it may be that he is.

"No," she said, "I have not been ill."

"Good. Are you ready now for another daiquiri?"

"Yes, please."

"Carl?"

"All right."

They had two new daiquiris and a Scotch, and Lisa sustained the lift, and it became night. Avery and Gail talked about things that had happened at the University when they were there and about things that had happened to them since they'd been there, and Lisa listened for a while and then began to think about things that had happened to her, but this threatened the lift, so she began listening to the canned music and watching the formulistic people. And after quite a while Carl asked her if she would like to have dinner, and she said she thought that she would.

Carl turned to Avery. "You'll have dinner with us, of course."

"Oh, no, thanks. I've intruded long enough."

"It's no intrusion at all. We'd love to have you, wouldn't we, Lisa?"

"Of course." Carl and Avery were both looking at her as if something more were expected of her, so she added, "Please join us. We're only going into the dining room here."

"Well, I'll accept on one condition. I pick up the check."

"That isn't necessary," Carl said.

"I insist. I can't accept unless you agree."

"All right." Carl shrugged and finished his last daiquiri in a gulp. "If you put it that way."

They got up and went out of the bar and into the dining room and were escorted to a table. An orchestra was playing something with a Latin rhythm, and a few couples were dancing at one end of the room on the small dance floor directly in front of the elevated place where the orchestra sat. The opposite end of the room was open to the terrace, and a few couples were dancing out there too.

"What are you going to have?" Carl said.

Lisa looked at the menu, and Avery said, "I'm going to have the pompano. It's very good."

"I think I shall too," Carl said. "It's something different. You don't often get pompano at home."

"There's a place in Corinth that serves it now and then. Em Page's restaurant."

"Really? That's rather surprising. It must be a pretty good place."

"It is. Em built it up from practically nothing, and he's very proud of it. It takes pride to make something good."

"Come to think of it, that's true. Pride works wonders."

"I'll also have the pompano," Lisa said.

Looking up from the menu, she saw that Avery was watching her with an odd intentness. He was apparently on the verge of saying something to her and was struggling against an impediment of some kind, just as a stammerer will hang up sometimes on a particular sound. The orchestra had begun a medley of tunes with a simple rhythm that required no mastery of intricate steps, and she understood suddenly that he was about to ask her to dance, and she wished that he wouldn't. Not, however, that she really felt strongly about it. She would prefer not to dance, but if he asked her, she decided, she would accept. She was feeling, as a matter of fact, quite assured. The certainty that she could cope with the small initial contacts of a normal routine filled her with inordinate pride.

"Would you care to dance?" he said.

"If you like. I'm not very good, though."

"Neither am I. I can only manage the simplest steps. If the orchestra gets off on a mambo or anything like that, I'll have to capitulate."

They stood up and threaded their way among tables to the dance floor and began to dance. He held her loosely, their bodies brushing lightly, and she was grateful for this. Neither did he try to talk with her, and she was grateful for this too. She moved gracefully, following his lead with ease, but in her grace there was a kind of paradoxical rigidity, as if it developed from the movement of her body as a unit and not from a harmony of parts. When the music ended, they returned to the table and found Carl beginning on his salad.

"Thank you," she said to Avery.

"Not at all. It was my pleasure."

Which was not true. He had obviously not enjoyed the dance and had only asked her out of courtesy. She recognized this and was not in the least disturbed by it.

They sat down and began eating their own salad. After a while the waiter brought the pompanos on a little cart and boned them beside the table and poured melted butter over them. Carl had ordered a bottle of sauterne. The waiter poured the sauterne and served the pompanos and went away. The sauterne was mediocre, Lisa thought, but the pompano was very good. It worked, however, against the lift. As a kind of depressant. She was beginning to feel imperiled, her assurance slipping, and she wished for another drink. As a drink, the sauterne was unsatisfactory. She sat with her hands folded in her lap and wished for a strong daiquiri.

"Won't you reconsider your condition?" Carl said. "About the check, I mean."

Avery shook his head. "No. I insist on the terns of the agreement."

In response to a signal, the waiter brought the check and left it on the table on a small tray. Avery picked up the check and examined it and put it back on the tray with a bill. He always tipped about fifteen percent and knew that the bill would just about cover it. His ability to compute rapidly in his head was something he was secretly proud of, and at the same time he was secretly ashamed of the pride. It was such a little thing, after all, to feel so strongly about.

"How about a drink on the terrace?" he said.

"No, thanks." Carl pushed his chair back. "I'm pretty tired, really. Guess I'm not fully recovered from the pneumonia. I think I'll go up to bed, if you'll excuse me. Perhaps I'll read for a while."

He was clearly making no impromptu excuse. His tiredness was evident in the ravishments of his face, the ruts and shadows and gray flesh, and even in the quality of his voice, which had developed a soft windiness, each word expelled with an effort on a slight burst of breath. Standing, he brushed a hand over his thin, fair hair. Avery stood too and helped Lisa.

"Must you run off too?" he said. "Could I interest you in another daiquiri?"

She did not want to remain alone with him, but on the other hand she wanted the drink very badly. She said that she would stay because the drink and the company seemed in present circumstances to be con-comitants.

"If it's all right with you," she said to Carl.

"Of course. I want you to enjoy yourself."

He looked at her in a way that seemed to suggest a significance under the surface of his words that was vastly greater than their literal meaning, and she thought, after he had said good-night and was walking away, that he had meant to be subtly compelling, that he was actually urging a conversion from aberrance to orthodoxy. She wondered if he understood the enormity of such a conversion, the perils entailed, and she was sorry for him and frightened for herself, and again she was conscious of a dry inner weeping.

"I would like that drink very much," she said.

They went into the bar and got the drinks and carried them out onto the terrace. The beach and the ocean were bright in the moon, and on the bright beach between her and the bright ocean were the appropri-ate bright people. Washed in moonlight, they were like characters in a phantasy. They were not real, she thought. They did things to one another and with one another and were very gay in their phantasy world, and they filled her, in spite of their quality of unreality, with fear and a convic-tion of proximate personal disaster. She had completely lost her recent assurance, and she wished suddenly and bitterly that she had stayed in Midland City with Bella. With Bella there was no security and no salva-tion, but there was at least the semi-peace of acceptance and submission.

She finished her daiquiri quickly and said, "I am tireder than I thought. I think I had better go upstairs after all."

"Must you really?"

"I think I had better."

"In that case, I'll see you to the elevator."

"No. Please don't bother. I thank you very much for everything."

"Not at all."

"Well, good-night, then."

In unconscious conformity to accepted ritual, she held out a hand, and he accepted it briefly, and she was aware again of the dry, hard inoffensiveness of his touch. Turning, she crossed the terrace and the lobby inside and went up in the elevator. In her room, she undressed and wished for another drink and thought that she would remember to buy a bottle to keep in the room tomorrow. Lying in bed, she could not see the bright sand and water below, but she could hear the roar of the surf, and the sound without the sight had a mood of its own and its own effect upon the mind, and after a while she thought of a phrase she must have read somewhere at some time: *the vast edges drear and naked shingles of the world*. The words had the quality of poetry, and they repeated themselves in her mind, but she could not remember where they came from or who had written them, and eventually she went to sleep.

SECTION 3

Down the beach a fat woman was sitting in a canvas chair under a large umbrella. The chair and the umbrella were matching pieces with alternating stripes of crimson and yellow. The woman was reading a book through the dark lenses of a pair of sunglasses, and every once in a while she would look up from the book and lift the glasses a little and stare out under them at a small girl who was playing in the sand about fifteen feet away between her and the water. The child was a skinny little thing with an incredible number of points and sharp edges. She had sparse red hair, a very light shade of red, almost pink, and it had been curled to make it look thicker than it was, but the effect had been only to make it look frizzled and brittle and no thicker at all. She was building little mounds of sand to represent buildings and tracing a path among the mounds to represent a road, and she was obviously bored with it and wishing for something more exciting to do. Sometimes she would stop what she was doing and look down the slope of the beach to the water, and then she would turn and look up the slope of the beach to the woman, but every time she looked at the woman, the woman was reading, or pretending to read, and the child would return to the buildings and road. Her imagination could instill no reality in them. They simply bored her, and what she really wanted was to go swimming in the ocean.

After quite a while the child got to her feet and walked up the beach to the woman and stood looking at her. She had learned from experience that this was an almost infallible technique in securing attention, and that the person so stared at would eventually respond, though not always in a way to be desired. The woman continued to look at her book, obviously trying to ignore the child, but signs of irritation were quickly apparent in a tic-like twitching of one corner of her mouth and in a turning of pages much more rapidly than they could possibly have been read. Conceding defeat, she lay the book face down in her lap and lifted the dark sunglasses, staring back at the child. She had difficulty sometimes in believing that this thin, homely girl was actually her daughter, had actually been conceived and nourished and issued in and by her own lush body, and if it had not been for a memory of pain that she had vowed would never be repeated she would have discounted the possibility entirely. Was it possible, she often wondered, that they had mixed things up in the hospital nursery?

"Yes, darling?" she said.

Her voice was heavy with imposed patience. The impossible child stared at her solemnly and kicked sand. "May I go swimming now?" she said.

"No, darling. You know I won't permit you to go swimming by yourself. You might be drowned."

"You could come with me."

"Not now, darling. Perhaps later."

"That's what you said a long time ago."

"It wasn't a long time ago. It only seems like it."

"Well, that's the same thing. It's the way things seem that's important."

"Please, darling. Don't argue."

"I'd like very much to go swimming. I wouldn't drown. I'd stay in the shallow water."

"No, darling. You know how Mother worries."

The woman lowered the sunglasses over her eyes and her eyes to the book. She stared at the open pages, comprehending nothing, conscious of the girl staring at her. After another minute, the girl turned and walked away, and the woman sighed with relief. The symbols on the pages resumed their assigned meaning, establishing relationship with one another, and she began to read.

The girl returned to the place where she had been, playing in the sand. Deliberately, with one naked foot, she leveled the buildings and obliterated the road. Turning, she looked up the beach at the man who was lying; there in the sun on his back with one arm bent up and over to protect his eyes. The man had come there about twenty minutes ago and had lain down and had been lying there without moving ever since. She wondered if he was asleep. If he went to sleep in the hot sun, he might be badly burned. He looked nice. He was not very young, but on the other hand neither was he very old, which was quite apparent in spite of the gray in his hair just over his ears. His body was slender and lightly tanned and didn't have any ugly overlap of flesh at the belt of his swimming trunks. She wondered if he would be willing to talk with her if she were to go up and introduce herself. Quite apart from that, however, it was possibly her duty to go and see if he were actually asleep and in danger of being badly burned. She threw a look over her shoulder at her mother and then walked up to where the man was lying. She stood looking down at him, and she began to think that the technique was not going to work for once, that the man was actually asleep, because it took him such a very long time to respond.

Eventually, however, he did. He stirred and lowered his arm and opened his eyes and looked up at her, and she waited patiently to see if he was going to be annoyed or indifferent or friendly. As it turned out, he didn't seem to be any of those things. He seemed merely curious.

"Hello," he said.

"Hello," she said. "My name is Eugenie."

"Is it? Mine's Avery."

"Were you asleep?"

"No. I was just lying with my eyes closed."

"I thought you might be asleep. You hadn't moved for so long, I mean. It's dangerous to sleep in the sun."

"I know. It was kind of you to be worried about it."

"Well, to tell the truth, I wasn't. Not very, anyhow. I just thought you might be willing to talk with me." He sat up, brushing the sand off his shoulders with one hand. Taking this as an invitation, or at least a kind of concession, she sat down in the sand facing him.

"Why do you want to talk?" he said.

"Because I'm bored."

"Bored? I didn't think girls your age ever got in than condition."

"Well, you're wrong. I'm very frequently bored."

"That's too bad. Can't you find anything to do?"

"What I really want to do is go swimming."

"Why don't you, then?"

"Because my mother won't let me. She's a terrible coward about the water. She's afraid I may be drowned."

"That isn't very likely if you stay in shallow water."

"I know. That's what I tell her, but it doesn't do any good. She said she might go with me later, but she probably won't. She always says that just to get me to stop asking, but she hardly ever does. She doesn't like the water."

"Is that your mother under the umbrella?"

"Yes. Reading the book."

At that moment the woman looked up and lifted the sunglasses. Missing the girl, she sat up suddenly. "Eugenie," she called.

The girl turned her head in the direction of the voice. "Here I am, Mother."

"You mustn't bother the gentleman."

"I'm not bothering. He said he would like to talk." This wasn't quite the truth, and she looked quickly at Avery from the corners of her eyes to see if he would support her in the small lie, and was relieved to see that he was looking at her mother and nodding his head.

"It's quite all right," he called.

Satisfied, the woman settled back in her chair again. She lowered the glasses and lifted the book. The girl turned back to Avery.

"Thank you," she said.

"Not at all."

"It wasn't quite true, you know. You didn't actually *say* you would like to talk."

"Didn't I? I want to, just the same. I guess I was getting bored myself."

"Do you get bored frequently?"

"Oh, I don't know. Sometimes."

"I do. I get bored *very* frequently. Are you married?"

"No."

"Neither is Mother."

"I beg your pardon?"

"She was married once but isn't any longer. She's divorced."

"That's too bad."

"Do you think so? I don't. I live part time with her and part time with Father. It makes things a little more interesting. It's not so boring when you change off."

"Where does your father live?"

"In Baltimore. That's in Maryland. My mother lives there too, but not with my father. They're divorced."

"I know. You told me that."

"I have a bad habit of repeating myself. Mother says I do, and I guess it's so. Why aren't you married?"

"I guess I just never found a girl who would have me."

She looked at him judicially, her head cocked to one side.

"I don't believe that's the reason at all. You're very good-looking you know."

"Well, I didn't know, as a matter of fact. Thank you for telling me."

"Do you intend to get married?"

He was quiet for a long time, looking beyond her and far out across the glittering water. She was afraid for a minute that she had offended him. Her mother often told her that she was far too inquisitive. She did not want to offend him because she would then have to go back to being bored, and she wished there were a way to retract the question, but of course it was too late, just as it was almost always too late to do anything about something you'd put your foot in. She was vastly relieved when he laughed quietly and did not seem to be offended after all.

"I've been thinking about it," he said.

"When?"

"I really haven't decided. I haven't even asked anyone. Soon, per-haps."

"I don't ever expect to get married myself."

"No? Why not?"

"Because I don't suppose anyone will ever want me. I'm too plain."

"Oh, I wouldn't say that."

"Well, if you wouldn't, it's just because you're kind. It's true, how-ever. I'm very plain, but I've learned to accept it. I've even learned to like it, rather. Being plain has advantages, you know. People don't expect so much of you."

"How old are you?"

"Ten. Why?"

"I just wondered. To tell the truth, I think a great deal should be expected of you. For ten, you're pretty precocious."

"Precocious? What does that mean?"

"It means that you act older than your age."

"Oh. My father has said the same thing, only he didn't use that par-ticular word. Would you care to go swimming?"

"I thought your mother wouldn't let you go."

"That was alone. I'm sure she'd allow it if you went too. Then she wouldn't have to take me later, you see. She hates going into the water."

"All right, then. You run over and ask, just to be certain."

The girl got up and went over to her mother, and Avery stood and watched the sequence of small actions between the two of them, the girl standing and waiting for attention, the mother lifting her eyes and lowering her book and glancing quickly, after listening for a moment, in his direction. Finally, the short nod of her head that signified assent, the relieved retreat to the book.

The girl returned and said, "I told you. It's perfectly all right."

"Good. I'll race you to the water."

She turned and ran down across the sand on thin, stem-like legs, and he followed more slowly, letting her stay ahead. When she reached the water, she went straight in, throwing her negligible weight against massive fluid resistance, and he increased his speed, catching up with her when the water was already above her waist.

"Can you swim?" he said.

"No."

"Then I don't think we'd better go any farther out."

She looked up at him. The salt water had splashed up and wet her hair, darkening the shade of red a little but making it look thinner than ever, and he thought that she was indeed an extremely homely little girl, but at the same time there was a strange, inquisitive charm about her.

"It would be all right if you were to carry me," she said.

"Yes, I suppose it would."

"If you'll just squat down a little I can get onto your back."

He turned and squatted down to make his back available, and she climbed quickly aboard. Her thin arms around his neck felt as if they had no flesh whatever on them. They were like flexible bone. He walked on out against the resistance of the Atlantic until only his head and neck were above water, and then she slipped off his back, retaining a hold on one arm.

"Help me float," she said.

She floundered over onto her back and began to sink, and he put a hand under her and raised her to the surface, and she lay there as rigidly as a body with rigor mortis, floating on the light touch of his fingers. Her weight, which was little enough normally, was hardly anything at all in the water. Apparently all she wanted to do was to lie on her back and look up into the sky, and she lay there on his fingers without speaking or moving, except as she was moved by the motion of the water, for what seemed to him like a very long time. Eventually he glanced toward the beach and saw the fat woman, her mother, standing at the edge of the water and gesturing for them to come in.

"Your mother wants you," he said.

"Yes." She closed her eyes and made a face at the sky. "I thought it must be about time. She never lets me stay in longer than fifteen or twenty minutes. It's a ridiculous idea of hers."

"Shall we go in, then?"

"I suppose we have to."

She flopped over onto her stomach and regained her hold on his arm. From there she clambered onto his back again, and he waded in with an exhilarating sense of power rising within him in a kind of counter-action to the descent of the water on his body. He felt like a god or something. Or like a saint. Saint Christopher rising from the water with a child on his back.

The mother, seeing them approach, had returned to her chair and was preparing to leave the beach. Avery deposited the girl on the sand and said, "It looks like you're going to have to go. Thank you for letting me go swimming with you."

"Did you really enjoy it?"

"Yes. It was fun."

"Mother will say I've made a nuisance of myself again. She says I bother people."

"In my case, that isn't so. You tell your mother that."

"I'll tell her, but she won't believe it. You're very nice. I hope you marry a nice girl."

"Did I say I was going to get married?"

"You said you were thinking about it."

"Yes. So I did. I remember now."

He looked down at her, at her small ugly face beneath the ridiculous pink hair, and she assumed all at once in his mind a monstrous and un-reasonable importance, as if he were suddenly certain through intuition that she was a kind of strange oracle by the sea who had come to him for a purpose which he must at this moment, before it was too late, recognize and exploit.

"Tell me," he said. "Do you think I should get married?"

"Yes." She gave him again her judicial stare. "Because you're kind. Women like kind men. In the end it's more important than anything else."

The woman called sharply before he could answer, and the girl turned and started up the slope of the beach. Without stopping, she turned her head and said to him over her shoulder, "Good-by. I don't suppose I'll see you again," and he stood and watched her go until she reached her mother, and continued to stand and watch as she and her mother, the fat woman and the thin child of points and edges, went away together. What had she called herself? Eugenie? Was it possible that the child really had such an inappropriate name? He wanted to laugh. Sustaining the sense of exhilaration and power that had risen within him as he emerged from the water, he felt uplifted and assured. Everything was so simple, really. All the complexities and distortions and doubts and fears were susceptible to dispersion by the answer of a child, and everything was, after all, so very, very simple.

He lay on the sand again and thought of Lisa. With this one, he thought, it would be possible. Because her flesh is pale and cool and quiet to the touch, devoid of fevers and hot adherence, it would be possible with her and time and resolution to establish and sustain an adequate relationship. One thing is certain. It must be done now and with this woman, or never and with no one. How I know this is not clear, but it is quite clear at any rate that it is true, and I even believe that this odd, ugly child Eugenie was sent this afternoon to establish it. Lisa. Lisa Sheridan. Lisa Sheridan Lawes. I can give her my name with a thought of intimacy and feel no more than the slightest revulsion. And even this will pass. Even this vestigial scar of early trauma and distortion will pass in time, and it will pass in the brick house above the river on High Street in the town of Corinth, in the place where trauma happened and distortion began and grew. It is all a matter of forgetting and learning, and it is not too late, though it would be too late after this last chance, and I am certain that it can be begun now and accomplished hereafter with this one woman with the pale, cool flesh.

But capacity? Diminishment and depletion of revulsion is one thing, a good thing but a negative thing, and capacity is quite another, because capacity is a positive rather than a negative, something that must be felt and done rather than simply not felt and not done. This is different. This is vastly more difficult. But it *can* be learned. I am sure that it is all a matter of learning, once you have unlearned all that formed the impediment to learning in the first place. One thing at a time. First one step and then the next. Like learning to walk. It will not do to consider all problems and perils together. One at a time. One after another as they are met. Who was it said that we would all be overwhelmed and terrified if we were conscious of all the deadly perils that threaten us every minute of every day in even the most commonplace affairs? It was Schopenhauer, I think. Yes, I am certain of it. It sounds just like him, the gloomy bastard, and I will not think any more about Schopenhauer, either, because he depresses me. I cannot at this moment think of anyone who ever lived who could possibly be worse for me to think about than Schopenhauer.

I will think, instead, about last night. She was quiet and remote in an aura of physical frailty, and it was not bad, it was not bad at all in the lounge and later on the terrace, the best of all the nights in the last two weeks of nights, each a little better in its turn, each in its turn holding a little more securely the quality of peace and rightness and growing ease. A lot can happen in two weeks. It is remarkable how much can happen. In two weeks of nights, nations can fall and families can break and a man can enter, after a fashion, into a new relationship with himself. A man can lie, after that much time, on the hot sand under the hot sun and consider dispassionately, as he was not able to consider before, the social and biological essentials involved in the procreation of his kind and the preservation of his name. He can think of a certain woman and decide definitely to marry her.

Hot. He was enveloped in heat that fell upon him from the sun and rose around him from the sand. It was time to move. If he did not move, he would be burned, as the girl with pink hair, the ugly little oracle Eugenie, had come to tell him quite some time ago. Getting to his feet, he walked up across the beach to the terrace of the hotel and saw Carl Sheridan sitting at a table with a tall cold glass in his hand. He went over and sat down at the table. Carl looked across the table at him and smiled and made a small tintinnabulation with glass and ice.

"Hello," he said.

"Hello. What's that you're drinking? It looks good."

"Just a Tom Collins."

"Gin. I never cared much for gin."

"It's all right when it's hot. When the weather's hot, I mean, not the gin. It's refreshing."

"I think I'll try one."

He started trying to catch the attention of a waiter. After a while he caught it and gave the order.

"Have you been swimming?" Carl said.

"Yes. I took a little girl out. Her name was Eugenie."

"Someone you know?"

"No. She was on the beach with her mother. She cane over and started talking with me and asked me to take her out."

"You look a little red, old boy."

"Do I? I lay on the sand for a while. Too long, I guess."

"You ought to be careful about that. You can get burned before you know it."

The waiter brought the Tom Collins. Avery picked it up and drank some of it. The glass was cold in his hand, and the Collins was cold in his throat, and Carl was right about it. It was pretty refreshing.

"We're leaving Saturday," Carl said. "Has Lisa told you?"

"No. She hasn't said anything about it."

"Oh? I thought perhaps she had."

"No, she hasn't said anything."

"Well, that's right. Saturday."

"I'm sorry to hear it."

"Sorry to leave, for that matter. But all good things must end, as the saying goes. I want to get home before Christmas."

"Are you feeling better now?"

"Oh, yes. Much. Quite thoroughly recovered."

"Lisa will go back with you, of course."

"Yes. Of course."

"Lisa and I have been together quite a lot since you introduced us. Every night, as a matter of fact."

"I know. I'm sorry to break it up, old boy."

"She's very charming."

"Do you think so? She'll be pleased to hear it."

"I have been thinking that I'd like to marry her. As her brother, would you object to that?"

"Not at all. Quite the contrary. I'm familiar with your background, of course. Your family and situation and all that. Have you asked her?"

"No. Not yet."

"Have you definitely decided to do so?"

"Yes. I'm not returning to Corinth until spring. Plan to go on to Mexico City in a couple weeks or so. I'd like to take Lisa with me."

"Marry her here, you mean?"

"That's right. Before you go back north, naturally."

"Well, it's up to her, old boy."

"I have your permission to ask her, then?"

"Certainly. And best of luck."

"Thanks."

Avery finished his Tom Collins and stood up.

"See you later," he said.

He went inside and up in the elevator. So this is the way you do it, he thought. This is the way you refute the past and imperil the future. In a few minutes. In a few words. As if it were nothing at all.

In his room, he showered and shaved and dressed. Already regret was working at him, the grave, reflective doubts. He thought of the odd little oracle of the afternoon, but she was now no more than an ugly child with no authority, and he went for his Scotch and found the bottle empty. Going to the telephone, he ordered another bottle and sat down to wait for it. When the bottle arrived in the hands of a bellhop, he paid the bellhop and poured three fingers and sat down again. He drank the Scotch a finger at a time and began to feel better.

SECTION 4

She was lying on the bed, just lying there quietly on her back and looking up at the ceiling and trying not to think about the wrong things, when someone knocked on the door. She continued to lie without moving until the knocking had stopped and started again after an interval, and then she got up and took an empty glass and a half-empty bottle of whiskey off the bedside table and carried them into the bathroom. Returning without them, she went to the door and opened it, and Carl came in.

"How are you, Lisa?" he said.

"All right. I was resting."

"I'm sorry I disturbed you."

"You know I didn't mean that."

He could smell the whiskey on her breath, and it bothered him. If she drank to excess in the bar or in company, he thought nothing of it, but when she drank in her room he immediately began to worry, because it seemed to him that solitary drinking was a bad sign. He walked over to the glass wall and stood with his back to her.

"I'd like to talk honestly with you, Lisa."

"I've been honest with you, Carl. I made up my mind to be, and I've been."

"I know. I believe you have. How are you feeling?"

"Most of the time I feel good. Sometimes depressed. Not for any particular reason. It's just something I can't help."

"Are you depressed now?"

"A little."

"What have you been thinking about?"

"Nothing much. I've been trying not to think at all."

"We're returning north Saturday, you know."

"Yes, I know."

"What will you do when you get there? Have you thought about that?"

"I've thought about it, but I don't know. I guess I'll get an apartment and a job and go on living."

"I'll help you financially, of course. But that isn't the first consideration. Will you be safe?"

"Safe? I'm not sure I know what you mean."

"Yes, you do. I mean, will you go back to the other life?"

"I don't know."

"I wish you would be a little more certain about it."

"I would be more certain if I could, but I can't. I don't know."

"I am willing to pay for a psychiatrist if you think it will help. Do you think it would?"

"I don't know about that, either. It might help, but I don't know."

He turned away from the window and came over and took her by the arms from the front and looked into her eyes.

"I love you, Lisa. I have always loved you in spite of everything, and I'm very worried about you."

"I know that. I didn't know it before, but now I do. It makes me want to cry, but I find that I am no longer able."

"Do you trust me?"

"Yes."

"Would you be willing to follow my advice?"

"I would be willing to try."

He released her arms and went over to a chair and sat down.

"I was just talking to Avery Lawes on the terrace."

"Oh?"

"You've been seeing Avery often, haven't you?"

"Every night. Sometimes in the day. I thought you wanted me to. I know you never said it, but I had the feeling you wanted it."

"So I did. I had the idea you would benefit from a normal relationship."

"That's what I thought you thought."

"Well, how do you feel about him?"

"I don't feel anyway about him. Neither one way nor another."

"You aren't repelled by him?"

"No. He's all right to be with. He doesn't disturb me."

"Perhaps that's a good sign."

"Perhaps."

"It might be the beginning of something more positive, I mean. He comes from an extremely good family."

"That's what you said."

"He's quite wealthy, I believe. He's the last of the family, too. He lives by himself in a large house. His father died only last summer."

"He told me that."

"Yes. Well, as I said, I was just talking to Avery on the terrace. The truth is, he is going to ask you to marry him."

"When?"

"Probably tonight. He wants the marriage performed before I leave on Saturday. How do you feel about it?"

"Terrified."

"Why? There's no need for that."

"Isn't there?"

"Oh, I know what you mean. You mean you will not be able to function as a wife. But you will. I'm convinced of that. At first it will be only a matter of submission, of compelling yourself to accept him passively, but later you will learn to find pleasure in him. In your relationship. It's normal, Lisa. It's the way men and women are supposed to be. Surely, if you give yourself the chance, it will be easier after a while to be normal, the way you're supposed to be, than to be the way that was never intended. That's only common sense."

"If only it were so simple."

"You must have a chance, Lisa. And to have a chance, you must *take* a chance. You would have wealth and a fine home. You would have a high position in society and would be respected automatically. It would be a kind of asylum for you. It would give you a chance to make the necessary conversion and to become well."

"We're forgetting something, aren't we?"

"What?"

"Avery. Doesn't he deserve some consideration? It seems like a dirty trick to play on him. To use him this way."

"He's asking of his own will."

"That's not the point, Carl. You know it isn't."

"It won't be a dirty trick if you make him a good wife."

"I'm not at all sure I can make him a good wife."

"You can. You must believe that you can."

"He will know something is wrong the first time we are together."

"Nonsense. He will only think you are frightened and inexperienced. Perhaps somewhat frigid. Many women are like that at first."

"I don't know, Carl."

He got up and took her by the arms again.

"I will tell you something. I will be perfectly frank. I don't really care a damn about Avery. I am not concerned about him. It is you I'm concerned about. I am willing to ruin him if it is a means of saving you. However, I do not think he will be ruined. I think it will work out for both of you. It is your chance, Lisa, your best and maybe your last chance for the asylum that is necessary in the beginning. You said you trusted me. You said you would try to follow my advice, and now I am asking you to try."

"Marry Avery?"

"Yes. Will you do it?"

"If you want me to."

"I do."

"All right. I will do it for you."

"Not for me. For you. That's the way you must think of it."

"For me, then. I will do it for me."

He leaned forward suddenly and kissed her on the cheek. His lips on her cool flesh felt dry and hot. "Perhaps I shall see you later downstairs," he said. Turning, he went over to the door and let himself out, and she walked into the bathroom and got the glass and the whiskey and brought them back and poured some of the whiskey into the glass and drank it. Then she lay down on the bed again and tried to relax completely and make her mind a blank. She was not able to accomplish this completely, but was at least partially successful, and she lay there for a long time, well over an hour, before she got up and went into the bathroom again and stripped and took a cold shower and then, after drying herself, brushed her teeth thoroughly with a dentifrice that was supposed to kill all odors on the breath, including the odor of whiskey.

When she was dressed, she went downstairs and out onto the terrace and stood by the balustrade looking down across the beach to the ocean. The hard glitter of the day was gone, and the air was softening and darkening, and the water beyond the beach was a vast shadow shifting uneasily in the cavities of the earth. She was cold, very cold, but the coldness was something that originated inwardly and had nothing to do with the descent of the sun, and was nothing that she could do anything about, except, perhaps, to get a drink as soon as possible. She did not go into the bar, however, but remained standing by the balustrade until Avery came up from behind and stood beside her.

"Here you are," he said.

"Yes. I've been waiting for you."

"Am I late?"

"No. I don't think so. I came down early."

"Would you like to have dinner?"

"I'm not hungry. I'm sure I couldn't eat a thing. Don't let me interfere with your own dinner, though."

"It's all right. I'm not hungry, either."

"Really? I'll go and sit with you if you wish."

"No, really. I'm not hungry at all. I'd prefer not to eat."

"In that case, I would like a drink."

"How would you like to go someplace different? I have been to a place I liked. A small place. It's quieter."

"All right. But first I would like one for the road."

"Fine. That's a good idea."

They went into the bar and had a drink and then went out into the lobby and waited until the Caddy was brought around. In the Caddy, they started for the other place he'd been to and liked. She sat in her corner of the seat and said nothing and reminded herself over and over that she had made a promise to Carl and that it was necessary for her own sake, as well as for the sake of abstract ethics, to keep the promise. The drink she'd just had was of some value in helping her face this necessity, but it was inadequate on the whole and wouldn't last and would soon need the assistance of another.

They came to the place they were going to, and it was small, as he'd said. And as he'd said, quiet. There were some tables and chairs and half a dozen booths and a bartender and a waitress and very little light. It was obviously a place to go and drink and talk if you wanted to, and if you had anything in mind besides drinking and talking, it was much better to go someplace else. They went in and got across from each other in a booth and began drinking, and pretty soon they began talking. "Have you talked to Carl?" he said.

"At lunch."

"Not since then?"

"No," she lied. "Not since lunch."

"I saw him on the terrace of the hotel this afternoon. Late. I had just come up from the beach. He told me you are returning north this Saturday."

"Yes. He wants to be home by Christmas."

"I'm sorry."

"So am I. I would like to stay here all winter."

"In Miami?"

"Not particularly in Miami. Somewhere in the sun and the warmth. I would like never to have to live in the cold again."

"I'm going to Mexico City soon. Did you know that?"

"Carl may have mentioned it. I don't remember."

"Have you ever been in Mexico City?"

"No."

"It doesn't get as warm there as it does in Miami, but on the other hand it doesn't get cold, either. The nights are cool, and a topcoat is necessary, but the days are pleasant."

"You sound as if you'd been there."

"I was there once. A long time ago."

"Did you see a bullfight?"

"No. I was only a child. All I can remember is Chapultepec Park."

"I don't think I'd want to see a bullfight."

"I guess they're pretty brutal."

"It's not so much that. I think they would be dull."

"They sound interesting enough in Hemingway."

"Everything sounds interesting in Hemingway. It's the way he writes."

"Perhaps I'll see one while I'm there. It would be interesting to find out, anyhow."

"Do they have them in winter? Is there a season for them, or do they have them the year around?"

"I don't know. I never thought about it, to tell the truth."

"How long will you stay there?"

"Until spring."

"Will you go home then?"

"Yes. Back to Corinth. Have you been in Corinth?"

"Once. I don't remember much about it."

"There's not much to remember. It's not much of a place."

"Why don't you tell me about it?"

"Well, it's just a town. I was born there, and I've lived there all my life, and I expect I'll die there. My mother is dead, and my father is dead, and I live alone in a brick house on High Street above the river that my family has lived in for four generations. I've thought about going away to live in some other house in some other town, but if I did I'd probably spend the rest of my life wishing I hadn't and wanting to go back."

"You could go back if you wanted to, couldn't you?"

"Of course. And I would. So it's much simpler not to go away at all. Except for a while at a time, like now. I'll go to Mexico City and see Chapultepec Park again, and maybe a bullfight, and then I'll go back. Some other time I'll go some other place. And back. Always back."

Their glasses were empty, so he signaled the waitress, and she came and took them away and brought them back full. He took a drink and looked at her and thought how cool her pale flesh looked and how her loveliness was something almost detached, something related in only the most incidental way to flesh and bone and the arrangement of features.

"I've been wondering something," he said. "I've been wondering if you would care to come with me."

"To Mexico City?"

"Yes. And then back to Corinth. I've been wondering if you would care to marry me."

"I doubt that you want me to marry you, really."

"I do, though. I've thought about it very carefully, and I've decided."

"It's a fine compliment. Thank you very much."

"Does that mean you will do it?"

"If you're sure it's what you want."

"I'm sure. I tell you I'm sure."

"Perhaps, before we make it definite, I had better tell you something about myself."

"Don't tell me anything you don't want to."

"But I want to. I want to tell you that I will make a very unsatisfactory wife. This is because I have no desire for you. If we are married, I will try to learn to desire you, but I doubt that I can ever learn. It is not only you, you understand. It is a deficiency in me in relation to all men."

"You mean you are frigid?"

She considered the truth but could not tell it, and so she told the lie.

"Yes. I'm sorry. And now you can retract your proposal, and we will have some more drinks and forget all about it."

He looked down into his glass, and she could see that his shoulders had begun to shake, and she thought with horror that he was crying, but then after a moment she saw that he was not crying but laughing, and this only increased her horror because the laughter contained this arid agony of hysteria and was far worse than the crying would have been. Without thinking, in her urgent need to stop him, she reached across the table and laid the fingers of one hand against the side of his face, and he looked up at once, the laughter dying in his throat.

"What's the matter?" she said. "Why are you laughing?"

"Forgive me. I was laughing because I'm a coward and have been relieved of the necessity of acting with courage."

"What? What do you mean?"

"Nothing. Nothing at all. I would still like very much for you to marry me."

"In spite of the way I am?"

"It doesn't matter. The way you are and the way I am are things that may change or may not change, but in the meanwhile we will go to Mexico City and back to Corinth, and eventually we will find out."

She could not look at him any longer. She folded her hands on the edge of the table and looked down at the hands and listened to the sound within her of the dry weeping.

"You are very kind," she said.

Which was an echo of the oracle, he thought.

Women like kind men, the oracle had said. In the end, she had said, it is more important than anything else.

He wondered if it was true.

SECTION 5

The night was alive, and all things in it. He lay in the center of the living night and was the focus of the living things. They crouched and waited and watched in darkness, and he rose and fell in silky, sickening motion on the breast of the breathing bed, and nothing happened, nothing at all.

Getting up, he moved among the living things and lit a cigarette and opened the blind at the window and admitted the slanting light of the circling moon. His body was wet, and the wetness evaporated in the air, and he was cold. Turning, he saw the other body, the white body in the white light, and it was perfectly still and from appearances might have been dead.

"It's all right," he said. "It doesn't matter."

"It's not all right," she answered. "It never will be."

"Eventually it will. It is something we can learn."

"You don't know. It's not the way you think it is."

"I know that we must be patient with each other."

"Do you really think it is so simple? I shouldn't have married you. It was a dirty trick that you didn't deserve."

"No. You told the truth. As you now know, that is more than I did."

"You think I told you the truth? Oh, well, it is too late to worry about that. It is too late for anything."

"You're just feeling depressed. Futility is always depressing, but you will feel better tomorrow. Can I get you something? A cigarette? A drink?"

"No, thank you. Nothing."

He left the window and lay down beside her on the bed. The living things had quit living and watching and waiting and had become the dead fittings of the room. Outside, the moon moved on.

CHAPTER IV

SECTION 1

Emerson usually handled the bar himself until Roscoe came in around eleven. Mornings were slack, and it was hardly worth hiring someone to do the job, and besides, Emerson liked to do a share of work around the place. It kept his hand in and gave him a good, solid feeling of personal intimacy with the things he had created and developed and loved. He was polishing glasses and looking through them against the light for smears when the postman came in.

"Well," he said. "The good man in gray."

The postman put his leather pouch on one stool and sat down on another. His name was Marvin Groggins, and he hated all people who wrote letters and was very proud of his casual rapport with all the business men on his downtown route, no matter how God-damn important they were, or thought they were.

"Crap," he said.

Emerson grinned. "What do you mean, crap? You better watch out, Marv, or you'll be getting investigated for subversive talk or something. You got to show proper respect for public servants, even if you happen to be one of them yourself."

"Oh, sure. Public servant. You know what I am? I'm a God-damn errand boy for a lot of fatheads, that's what I am. You see that bag? Look at it. Just look at the God-damn thing. Bulging. Running over. And you know something? I could take at least half of that stuff and throw it down the nearest storm sewer, and no one would be a damn bit the worse off for it, and the truth is, they'd probably be a hell of a lot *better* off."

"Except you, Marv. You'd be worse off. You'd be in the pokey, as a matter of fact."

"I know. Durance vile. Just for throwing away a bundle of lousy trash. I'm not so sure I'd be worse off, at that. You got to put up with a hell of a lot in this postman racket. Take Aunt Lucy, for instance."

"Who's Aunt Lucy?"

"Well, she's just a for-instance, damn it. The point is, she hasn't got anything worth while to do with herself, so she writes letters. She writes them to everyone in her lousy family right down to umpteenth cousins, and no one wants the letters, and probably don't even read them, and all they really want is for Aunt Lucy to mind her own damn business, but after they get the letters their lousy consciences won't let them alone until they've answered them, and the thing keeps going on in a vicious circle, and it's the postman who suffers. Trouble is, stamps are too damn cheap. If stamps cost more, there wouldn't be all this stuff to peddle. By God, I'll vote for the first guy who runs for president on a platform calling for dollar postage stamps, and I don't give a damn if he's a Republican or a Democrat or a Druid."

"Druid? Druidism's a religion or something, isn't it?"

"I don't know what it is, and I don't give a damn. All the guy has to do is advocate dollar stamps. Minimum, that is."

"You're pretty bitter this morning, Marv. What you need is a couple fingers on the house."

Marv shook his head. He had a long, lugubrious face with a big nose that was now bright red from the cold. Emerson liked to get him going when there was time to listen, and he knew damn well that Marv loved his job and wouldn't have traded places with the postmaster general.

"Not while I'm on duty," Marv said. "Everyone else can take time out for a little drink if he pleases, but if a postman takes a drink on duty it's a stinking crime or something."

"How about a cup of coffee?"

"Well, coffee's something else. Even a postman can have a cup of coffee, I guess."

"Okay. You can have the coffee now and come back on your own time for the drink."

"Thanks, Em. I'll do that."

"Meantime, while I'm getting the coffee, you can dig my mail out of that bag. I want to get it before you decide to take it out and throw it down the sewer. You take cream and sugar?"

"Hell, no. You know better than that."

Emerson went back to the kitchen and got the coffee and brought it into the bar. Marv had sorted out half a dozen envelopes, and Emerson set the coffee down in front of Marv and picked up the envelopes. He went through them slowly, reading the return address on each one.

"Well, I'll be damned!" he said.

Marv had his big red nose stuck down into the fragrant steam rising from the coffee. He rolled his eyes up at Emerson without removing his nose from the steam. "Bad news?"

"No. I don't suppose so. How the hell would I know, Marv? I haven't even opened the envelope."

"The way you sounded…"

"I was just surprised. It's from Mexico City, as a matter of fact. From Avery Lawes."

"Avery Lawes? I thought Avery went to Miami."

"He did, but apparently he went on to Mexico City later. He told me he might do that when he was in here the night before he left town."

"Some guys sure lead a hard life. I suppose he'll come back with the birds, after it gets nice and warm and everything. You a particular friend of Avery's?"

"Not particular. I've known him sort of casually ever since we were kids."

Emerson held the envelope against the light to locate the letter inside and tore a strip off the end of the envelope. Removing the single sheet of stationery, he began to read. The letter was very brief, only a note, and the reading required no more than half a minute. Marv lifted his coffee cup and drank from it and tried to act as if he wasn't interested. Emerson put the letter back into the envelope and began to laugh.

"What's funny?" Marv said.

"Nothing. Nothing's funny."

"What the hell you laughing for, then?"

"I was just thinking about something Avery told me once."

"Oh, well, pardon me all to hell. I certainly wouldn't want to intrude on a private joke. How's Avery managing to get along down there with all those Mexican gals and everything?"

"Fine. He's married."

"The hell you say!"

"That's right. He married a girl in Miami and took her to Mexico City with him."

"Well, I'll be! Imagine old Avery doing something like that. Maybe he got hooked. You think so? Sometimes when these highbrow guys get out of town on the loose, they really pop their corks."

"I doubt that Avery popped his cork."

"He never seemed like the kind that would. I'll admit that."

"He's not highbrow, either. Avery's a mighty nice guy when you get to know him."

"Hell, I didn't mean any offense. If you say so, Em, he's a ring-tailed wonder. He's the greatest guy in the world. Did he say who he married?"

"Yes. A girl named Lisa Sheridan. Apparently she's the sister of some fellow Avery knew in college. She's from Midland City. She and her brother and Avery got together down in Miami, and it was just a natural development from there, I guess. I'm glad for Avery myself. It was time he got married."

"Why?"

"What do you mean, why? Because he's thirty years old and the last of his family, that's why. Because a man needs a warm bed to get into at night, that's why."

"Nuts. A guy with Avery's dough wouldn't have any trouble finding someone to warm his bed for him. The truth of the matter is, it just drives a married guy crazy to see another guy who's had sense enough to stay single. Misery loves company, as the saying goes."

"Well, speaking of misery, you're just about the most miserable bastard I've seen in a long time, Marv. Maybe you better have a shot in spite of the rules."

"Nope. Can't do it, Em. Thanks just the same." Marv finished his coffee in a big gulp, his prominent Adam's apple jumping over the swallow, and stood up. "Got to be on my appointed rounds. Neither sun nor rain nor sleet nor snow, et cetera. Or something like that. See you tomorrow with another load of ads for bar supplies."

"Just so you don't bring anything from Aunt Lucy." Marv heaved his bag onto his shoulder and walked toward the front door. He was wearing galoshes, and the tops flopped together in passing with a harsh rasping sound. At the door he met Roscoe coming in.

"Hello, courier," Roscoe said.

"Crap," Marv said.

He went on out into the street on Aunt Lucy's business, and Roscoe walked back to the rear of the bar and hung his hat and overcoat and suit coat in a closet. From the same closet he removed a starched white jacket and put it on. Back in the old days, in the old owl diner, he'd been sloppy about his clothes, and his shirts had been more often soiled than not, but since he'd come to work as bartender for Emerson, there had been a complete reversal of this, and he was always scoured and polished and pressed until he looked positively antiseptic. He walked up behind the bar from the closet to where Emerson stood looking at the rest of his mail.

"Bills?" he said.

Emerson laughed and shook his head. "Too early for bills, Roscoe. Look for them next week."

"Just ads, I guess. Everyone selling something."

"Mostly. There's a letter from Avery Lawes."

"No kidding? Looks like he's adopted you or something. Didn't you get a card from Miami about a month ago?"

"Nearer six weeks. He's in Mexico City now."

"My God, isn't it awful to have money? Here we are, wading around in this God-damn slop, and Avery takes it easy in the sun. Wonder when he's coming home?"

"Early spring, probably. He said so in the letter."

"Nice. Gets cold, go away. Gets warm, come back. Well, I wish I could afford to do the same thing. Can't take the winters like I used to. When you get older, they get rougher. Can't shake the colds, somehow. I've had a snotty nose for three months."

"You been feeling bad? Why the hell didn't you say so? Anytime you're feeling bad, you knock off work, Roscoe. You hear me? Anytime."

"Who wants to knock off? As far as I'm concerned, this is the best place in the world to be. Right here in this bar. I hope I die here. Go out fast, before I know what's hit me, no regrets and no expectations, right here with this strip of mahogany between me and the world. Mahogany's nice, you know? Best wood there is. Only request I've got to make, Em, is to be buried in a mahogany box. Will you see to it?"

"You're tough as cowhide, Roscoe. I'll be six under long before you are."

"Not so, Em. How old do you think I am? Close to seventy, I'll tell you. I've damn near had my three score and ten. Biblical allotment, you know. The old pump has to work at things now. I can hear it breathing with its mouth open. Well, to hell with that. Anything new with Avery?"

"A wife."

"What?"

"You heard me. A wife, I said. He's got himself married."

"Jesus Christ, just wait until that news breaks!"

"Why? What happens?"

"Are you kidding? It's treason, that's what it is. When Avery got hitched, it was supposed to be with a Corinth gal. You know that. Among the mothers with eligible daughters there will be such a weeping and wailing and gnashing of teeth as hasn't been heard since the fall of Jerusalem."

"You think so? You can start listening for the first sounds, then, because I just told Marv Groggins, and you know what that means."

"Sure. If Marv had been living in 1775, Paul Revere wouldn't have had a chance. And where would that have left Longfellow? What the hell rhymes with Groggins?"

"Noggins, toboggans, floggin's."

"No fair dropping g's. Longfellow was a Harvard graduate. Wasn't he?"

"I wouldn't know. Anyhow, I think you're exaggerating a little. About the reaction to Avery's getting married, that is."

"Well, maybe. It may not be noisy, but it will damn sure be real. Foreigners are all right in their places, you know, but Avery Lawes' bed isn't one of the places where they're all right. Not with a license for it, anyhow. If I were Avery's wife, I'd be preparing myself for dissection. Who'd you say she is?"

"I didn't say. Her name was Lisa Sheridan, though, according to Avery's letter. She comes from Midland City."

"Native state, anyhow. That may help a little. How did it happen?"

"It was just a short letter. Just a note. All I know is, Avery knew her brother in college, and they happened to be staying in the same hotel in Miami. The girl and her brother were there together. I don't think Avery had ever met her before."

"I had an idea Avery was a confirmed bachelor. Like me. Anyhow, the best of luck to him. Good bedding, good breeding, good fortune."

"That sounds like a toast. Did you make it up?"

"Right in my old bald head."

"I'd like to drink it to him, Roscoe. To Avery and his new wife. In good bourbon."

"Old Taylor, Old Crow, Old Grandad?"

"You pick it and pour it."

Roscoe set out two glasses and reached for a bottle. "What's given you this sudden affection for Avery Lawes?" he said.

"Can't a man wish another man well in his marriage without being in love with him?"

"Sure, he can, Em. A guy like you wishes everyone well, because it's the way he's put together, but I've got a feeling this is a little more than that. It's almost you're worried about him. Like you're afraid he isn't going to have the luck you're wishing for him."

Emerson looked into the good bourbon and remembered the night he'd driven Avery home. He had remembered it often, and it bothered him, and he didn't like being bothered, and he wished there was some way to get it out of his mind for good and all. The trouble was, he couldn't lose the feeling that Avery had been appealing for help that night, and that he, Emerson, had given him none whatever. But what the hell! A guy all fouled up inside might need help, and he might need it bad, but Emerson Page was the last person on earth he ought to go to to try to get it. Emerson Page just wasn't any good at that kind of stuff, even if he tried, and the only kind of trouble he could understand a guy's having was something like going broke or getting arrested or having a fight with his wife.

"Did I ever tell you about the night I drove Avery home?" he said. "Last November, it was. The night before he left for Miami."

"I remember the night. You never told me anything about it, though."

"Actually, there isn't a lot to tell. He was just all wound up, that's all. But it didn't seem like something recent. You know what I mean. Not like something that had come in a hurry, over something in particular, and would leave the same way. It was something that had been building up in him for a long time. For years."

"Maybe he just needed what he found in Miami and took to Mexico City."

"Sure. That's probably it. Well, anyhow, here it is, Roscoe. To Avery Lawes and Mrs. Avery Lawes. Good bedding, good breeding, good fortune."

They touched glasses and drank the mellow bourbon. Roscoe took the glasses and dripped them in a solution of disinfectant and began to polish them. Through the archway in the dining room, the luncheon crowd had started to gather, and Emerson stood listening to the undulation of voices in the aggregate and the small, brisk sounds of service. Three men came in from the street and lined up at the bar, and Roscoe went to take care of them. He set out three bottles of Budweiser with glasses and returned to Emerson.

"It's almost noon. You having lunch now?"

"Pretty soon. I think I'll go up and see if Ed wants lo come down. She was asleep when I left this morning."

"Sure. You go see Ed. I'll handle things here. Give Ed my best."

"I'll do that. How about you? You had anything to eat?"

"Not yet. I'll grab a sandwich later."

"Want me to have one sent in from the kitchen?"

"If you don't mind. Make it roast beef."

"Right. See you later, Roscoe."

He went through the dining room, skirting the edge, and into the kitchen. After stopping long enough to give instructions about Roscoe's sandwich, he went on up the stairs to the apartment, reflecting on the way that it was really quite remarkable how he kept on feeling year after year when he was returning to Ed, even after a very short time of being away, not exactly excited, because excitement is something that is for very special occasions and would not be possible or desirable as emotional accompaniment for every small event, but quietly alive with a feeling of anticipation and eagerness and expectancy. You never quite knew with Ed. You never quite knew what would be next, but you knew, whatever it was, that it would be interesting.

He went into the living room, and she wasn't there, and so he crossed over to the bedroom door and looked in, and she was. She was dressed in a dark blue wool dress that fit her like a kid glove, and she was standing in front of the full length mirror on the back of the closet door, with her back to the mirror, and she was holding up the skirt of the dress and looking over her shoulder into the glass to see if the seams of her stockings were straight.

"They are," he said.

She saw him in the mirror and smiled and turned her head lazily.

"Hello, darling. What are?"

"Your seams. Straight, I mean."

"Yes. They do seem to be, don't they? The stockings are a new shade. Do you like them?"

"They're well-filled. I'll say that for them."

"Thank you. One of the very nicest things about you is the way you say flattering things with only the slightest prompting."

"With you, it's easy. Is that a new dress too?"

"I bought it a couple days ago. And don't ask how much it cost, because I won't tell you."

"Who's asking? All I want to know is, do you put it on or paint it on?"

"Really? Is it that tight?"

"I was just joking, darling. You have nothing to hide."

"Oh, you. Was I asleep when you left this morning?"

"You were. With your mouth open."

"That's a dirty lie. Malicious slander. I could sue you for saying that."

"For what? Divorce?"

"Well, no. I don't think I want a divorce. Not even separate maintenance. Just wife support, let's say. In return for a consistent and satisfactory performance of wifely duties, of course. I'll tell you what. Right now I'll settle out of court for enough to do some shopping with this afternoon."

"Agreed. I always like to keep these family hassles in the home, if possible."

He walked across to her dressing table, removing his billfold from the right hip pocket of his trousers as he went, and laid some bills on the glass top of the table beside her hair brush. She came over and picked them up and counted them and brushed his lips with hers for each bill.

"Thank you, darling."

"Not at all. You smell very good. I like that scent you're wearing. It's sharp and clean. There's a word to describe it, but I can't think of the word."

"Astringent?"

"That's it. Astringent. Isn't it lucky that I have a wife who reads too?"

"What's the exact implication of that *too*, man?"

"Well, do you cook? Do you sew? Shall I continue making an inventory of your talents?"

"Never mind. The trouble with you is, you have a distorted sense of values. You're just blind to all my other fine accomplishments."

"It's your fault. Once I was a clean lad with a pure mind, but you've corrupted me."

"Whoa! Down, boy! Let's think about lunch."

"That's what I really came up about, come to think of it, to see if you want to have lunch with your husband. However, I've been distracted. It always distracts me to see a wife in a new blue dress. There's sautéed chicken livers."

"Oh, good. That's what I'll have. Just give me time to go over my face lightly. Talk to me. Tell me what happened downstairs this morning."

"Nothing much. I handled the bar until Roscoe came in. Marv Groggins had a cup of coffee on the house and bellyached about Aunt Lucy."

"Marv Groggins has an Aunt Lucy? I find that incredible. I find it wholly incredible that Marv has any relatives at all. I assumed that he was born by a kind of spontaneous combustion in a rotten stump."

"Oh, Marv isn't so bad. Just windy, that's all. Anyhow, he doesn't actually have an Aunt Lucy. Aunt Lucy is just someone who stands for anyone who is sadistic enough to write a letter for some poor postman to peddle."

"I see. What's his solution? Slaughter Aunt Lucy and sell her to the glue factory?"

"No. Nothing so drastic. He only wants to charge her a dollar for a stamp."

"That figures. In Marv's little mind, almost anything figures. Did we get a letter from Aunt Lucy?"

"Not Aunt Lucy. Avery Lawes."

"You don't tell me. Has he got himself cleaned out? Wasn't that the way he put it?"

"Yes, that was the way. Apparently he's done a damn good job of it in a pretty short time. He's married."

"Is that so? Good for Avery. Blessings on him and everything."

"You don't seem very surprised about it."

"Why the hell should I be surprised when a man thirty years old gets married? It's something that could have happened any time."

"I mean, Avery being what he is and all. Or was. Or seemed. You remember what I told you about the night I took him home last November."

"That hocus pocus about the Mexican musician? How long does a man go on brooding about something that happened when he was a kid?"

"Maybe the Mexican business was just part of it. Incidentally, Avery and his wife are in Mexico City right now."

"Yes? Do you suppose there's a psychological reason for Avery's going back there? Something like a criminal returning to the scene of his crime? Well, maybe he'll stray off and have a female Mexican musician for himself, and that will fix everything up. Sort of cancel out the other time."

"That would be very neat."

"Wouldn't it? I like things to work out neatly. Do we know his wife?"

"No. Her name was Sheridan. Lisa Sheridan. She comes from Midland City."

"That close? It's funny, isn't it, how two people so near each other have to go all the way to Miami to meet?"

"I guess so. Lots of people go to Miami in the winter, though. The ones who can afford it."

He moved up behind her and put his hands on her shoulders. She stopped fooling with her lipstick and tipped her head back and looked up at him through her lashes.

"Sautéed chicken livers, you say?"

"Yes."

"Just keep them in your mind. Concentrate on them. Keep thinking about chicken livers, and you'll be perfectly all right. Darling, you're not concentrating."

"I'm trying, but it doesn't seem to be working."

"Damn it, Em, you're messing me up."

"Chicken livers, chicken livers, chicken livers. Why doesn't it work, Ed? What is this sudden madness that will not submit even to the thought of chicken livers?"

"Really, Em! After all this hard work! Oh, well, if you're going to do a job, you might as well do a good one. Mess me up good, darling..."

SECTION 2

In the established cycle of measured time, January came to February, February came to March, and Mr. and Mrs. Avery Lawes came to

Corinth. For the purpose of presenting the new wife, there was a party in the brick house on High Street to which people came who moved in the level of society that included the Laweses, which was top level and did not include Mr. and Mrs. Emerson Page. Not that Avery would have objected to including them or have had the slightest hesitation in inviting them if he had thought for a moment that they would have wanted to come, but he knew very well that they would not. He did not know Ed Page well and had no particular feeling about her one way or another, but for Emerson he had a natural liking that was stronger than any feeling he had for any other living man.

Avery had not entertained since becoming master of the High Street house, and the party limped, and the dissecting of Lisa proceeded with quiet deadliness and complete inaccuracy, and after the guests had crawled into their Buicks and Chryslers and Lincolns and Cadillacs and driven away, Lisa went upstairs to her room, and Avery got some ice and two glasses and a bottle of Scotch and followed her. He knocked on her door, and she told him to come in, which he did. It was the same room in which his father had once told his mother that it would possibly be a good idea to kill her.

"I thought you might like a nightcap," he said.

"I would," she said. "I would like one very much."

She sat erectly on the edge of the bed while he fixed the drinks. When he handed her one, she took it and held it in both hands, the hands cupped around the glass, and lifted it to her lips as if it were something very heavy. With his own in hand, he sat down carefully in a chair: and stretched his legs and thought, looking across at her, that her appearance of frailty was even more pronounced than usual and that she was surely, beneath her superficial surface rigidity, on the verge of collapse. She was still wearing the dress she had worn at the party, a white dress pinched in at her tiny waist and cut low in the bodice to reveal partially the upper slopes of her small breasts, and she looked very young, and he was very sorry for her.

"It was rather deadly, wasn't it?"

"Yes. I'm afraid I won't be very good at entertaining. Will we have to do it often?"

"No. Not at all if you don't want to."

"I will try to do it once in a while. I don't want to keep you from your friends."

"Nonsense. I wish you wouldn't talk like that. The truth is, I don't like this kind of thing myself. Are you very tired?"

She thought of the depressing party and, beyond the party, of the arid, passionless, exhausting Mexican nights that had achieved nothing, and she was certain that it would have been impossible for anyone to be more tired than she was at that moment.

"Yes," she said. "Are you?"

"Rather. I'll finish my drink and go away and let you rest."

"Don't hurry. You are welcome to stay as long as you like."

"Do you feel like talking a little?"

"If you want to talk, I'll talk."

"Tell me. How do you feel about it now? Now that we are settled in the house and you have met some of the people you will know?"

"Honestly?"

"Yes, of course. Honestly."

"I feel just as I have felt from the first. Just as I told you in Miami and later in Mexico City. I feel that I have done you a great harm that you did not deserve and that I have taken the first step toward ruining your life and that I had better leave before I ruin it entirely."

"That's really a joke, Lisa. That part about ruining my life. You have no idea how big a joke I find it. I've tried and tried to tell you that this thing which is impossible between us does not matter. It is simply of no importance. Without it, we can still make something for ourselves that will be solid and secure and good for both of us. Can't you understand that?"

"It is you who don't understand."

"Perhaps not. If I don't, I wish you would try to make ft me.

"I can't. It is something I simply can't do."

"Do you really want to leave me? If you really want it, I won't try to stop you, but I wish that you wouldn't."

"No. I remember what I promised you that particularly horrible night in Mexico City. Do you think I have forgotten? I promised that I would try for a year, and I will keep my promise. I will try sincerely."

He stood up and finished his drink standing, pretending a certainty that he did not feel.

"Good. It will work out for us in a year. I'm sure of that. I'm very fond of you, Lisa. Really I am. I should hate to lose you."

"I'm fond of you too. I'm rather surprised that I am, to tell you the truth, but nevertheless it is so. You are kind and patient and much too good for me."

"You mustn't say that. Believe me, I'm not too good for anyone." He turned and went to the door. "Tomorrow night I'd like to take you out to dinner. To Em Page's place. Will you go?"

"Of course."

"I think you'll like it there. It's quiet and comfortable, and the food's the best in town. I think you'll like Em too."

"You have mentioned this Emerson Page several times. Are you very old friends?"

"I don't think you could quite say that. I like him, that's all. He's a nice, simple guy who does things."

"I see. Well, I suppose there is a virtue in that. Doing things, I mean. Will you be home tomorrow?"

"Not until evening. Do you mind?"

"No, no. Of course not. I only wondered."

"Are you sure there is nothing I can do for you before I leave?"

"Quite sure."

"You look very tired. Why don't you sleep late in the morning?"

"Perhaps I shall."

"I believe I would, if I were you. Goodnight, now!"

"Goodnight."

As soon as he was gone, she got up immediately and went into the bathroom and undressed and showered and put on a nightgown. Returning to the bedroom, she was aware of the presence of the piece of bottle and wondered if he had merely forgotten it or had left it deliberately. In either case she was thankful, and she poured some of the Scotch over ice and sat down again on the edge of the bed and drank the Scotch slowly.

When the glass was empty, she turned out the light and lay down on the bed in the darkness and tried to achieve complete relaxation in a way she had learned and had sometimes found effective, but now it was impossible because she kept thinking in spite of herself of the sterile Mexican nights. Parallel to revulsion and despair, which were concomitants of the nights and remembrance of the nights, was the heretical hunger grown great in abstinence, and this was the oppressive menace, the presence of passion and not the lack of it, and it was this that Avery did not understand and that she could not explain, and it was this, she thought, that would surely b; in the end, the destruction of her, who deserved it, and perhaps of him, who did not. She was exhausted, but she could not sleep, and after a while she got up and had another drink and lay back down again, and a long time after that, near daybreak, she went to sleep at last and slept heavily until noon. During the afternoon she ate nothing and drank nothing and succeeded in thinking very little, and in the evening she went with Avery to Emerson Page's restaurant.

She liked it there, as Avery had thought she would, and she was glad she had come. From her position at a table across from Avery, she could look at an angle through an archway into the bar and see the back of a woman on a stool between the backs of two men on stools, and she could hear modulated canned music, and a drink, which she had denied herself all afternoon, was now permissible. A waitress came to take their order, and she told Avery to use his own judgment about dinner but that she would like a martini first of all, and he gave the order for the dinner and the martinis, and the waitress went off to the kitchen and returned immediately and went into the bar and returned from there with the martinis. Lisa sipped hers, which was very dry and good, and saw a man come through the archway from the bar and pause and look around and see them and make his way toward them among the intervening tables. He was an inch or two under six feet, with a compact body, and he walked with a slight limp. His face was rather dark-skinned and had a quality of boyish openness about it that made him look younger than he probably was, and she was absolutely certain, though she had never seen him before or heard him described physically, that this was Emerson Page, who was a nice, simple guy who did things. However, though her conviction of recognition was immediate and correct, it had in her mind no special significance and was accompanied by no particular emotional reaction. She watched him come with indifference.

Avery stood up and extended a hand and said, "Hello, Em. Good to see you again."

Emerson took the hand and released it. "Good to have you back, Avery. Nice winter? I guess I don't have to ask that, though. Congratulations."

"Thanks. And here she is, Em. My wife Lisa. Lisa, this is Emerson Page."

Emerson looked down at Lisa and smiled and made a minimal bow from the waist and said, "How do you do," with an appealing suggestion of shyness, and she responded and said that she felt like she already knew him because he seemed to be the only person in Corinth Avery ever mentioned.

"It that so?" he said. "I'm flattered."

"You have a very nice place. Avery said it was nice, and it is. I like it."

"Thank you. I hope you come often. How do you like Corinth by now? It must seem pretty small after Midland City and Miami and Mexico City and all those places."

"I haven't noticed. I don't think I will mind its being small."

He turned back to Avery. "I was at the bar when your letter came. The one saying you were married. Roscoe and I drank a toast to your happiness."

"Did you? That was a nice gesture, Em. I appreciate it"

Emerson lifted a hand as if he were going to put it on Avery's arm and then halted the motion before it was completed. The hand dropped to his side.

"Well, I won't intrude any longer. Just wanted to say hello. Has your order been taken?"

"Yes. Can't complain about the service."

"Good. I hope you enjoy your dinner and will consider yourselves as my guests for tonight."

"That's extremely generous of you."

Emerson smiled again at Lisa, the smile suggesting the same hesitancy that had interrupted and deflected his gesture toward Avery, as if he were uncertain of its reception.

"I'm pleased to have met you, Mrs. Lawes. I wish you much happiness."

"Thank you."

He walked away, the limp barely apparent as his weight descended on his right leg, and Avery sat down.

"Nice guy," he said. "Deserves a lot of credit. He was a poor kid, you know. I remember him delivering papers and parcels and things like that almost as far back as I can remember. He started this place on a shoestring and has made something of it."

"Is he married?"

"Oh, yes. Didn't I tell you that?"

"I don't remember that you did."

"His wife's name is Edwina. He calls her Ed. Quite a pretty woman, everyone seems to think. She'll probably be down later. They live in an apartment upstairs, and she often comes down. Perhaps you will meet her."

The martini in her empty stomach was having an immediate and powerful effect. Shapes and sounds were softened and subdued, had lost in minutes the effect of harsh or discordant impact on her senses, and the face of Avery, across the table, was the identification of someone she knew and rather liked and who was for the time being no particular problem. The world was reduced to the dimensions of a small restaurant in a small town, and the biggest problem in the reduced world was whether there was time before dinner for another martini, or granted the time, whether it was advisable to have it.

She thought that it would possibly be wiser to have dinner before the second martini, because the first martini was really having a remarkably potent effect, and it was not at all impossible that she might, at this rate, become quickly drunk. The thought of Mrs. Avery Lawes publicly drunk on her first night out in Corinth seemed to be a very good joke that amused her considerably, and she looked down at the olive lying naked in the thin shell of her martini glass and laughed quietly at the good joke.

"What's the matter?" Avery said.

"Nothing. Nothing whatever is the matter. I was only wondering if it would be advisable to have another martini while we are waiting for dinner."

"Well, I don't know. Maybe we should wait until afterward."

"All right."

"I don't want to be arbitrary about it, however. If you really want the martini, I'll get it."

"No. You are probably perfectly right. It would be better to wait."

"You know how it is sometimes on an empty stomach."

"Yes, I know."

"Are you sure it's all right? I don't want to be arbitrary."

"You said once that you didn't, and I believe that you don't. I am convinced that you are right in saying that we should wait until after dinner. Is that satisfactory? If it is, we can quit discussing it."

"Are you annoyed?"

"No."

"You sound as if you are."

"I am not annoyed. I just don't want to spend the rest of the night discussing whether we should have another martini or not."

He looked at her for a moment and then got up and walked into the bar and returned a few minutes later with a fresh martini. He placed it in front of her and sat down without saying anything, and she picked it up and drank some of it and wondered why she had been so nasty with him when she was actually feeling quite affectionate and not inclined to be nasty at all. Granted that it was irritating to want a martini and have it denied you, it was nevertheless nothing to warrant a quarrel, especially when the martini was not exactly being denied you, but was only being postponed for a while. "Thank you," she said.

"You're quite welcome."

"Have I made you angry?"

"No. Of course not."

"If I have, I'm sorry."

"Really I'm not angry. If you want a martini, it's your right to have one."

"I'm a nasty bitch."

"Don't say that."

"I am, though, just the same. You have been much too kind to me, and I repay you by being the nastiest kind of bitch."

"Look, Lisa. Please don't talk like that. Here. Let me have a sip of the martini, will you? I should have got another for myself."

She handed the glass across to him, and he took it and drank a little of the martini, and she was truly sorry for the way she had behaved. She was about to say so for the second time, but the waitress came at that moment with the dinner and prevented her. The second martini was verifying what the first had indicated, that it was essential to get some food into her stomach if she was to continue drinking, but the food was revolting and absolutely inedible, not because it was bad or badly prepared, but simply because it was food, and she ate some salad and a bite or two of meat and could force herself to eat no more.

"Aren't you hungry?" Avery said.

"I don't seem to be. I thought I was, but the sight of the food has taken away my appetite."

"It's very good."

"I don't doubt it. It's not that. It's nothing to do with the way the food is prepared or anything."

"You ought to eat more, Lisa. You eat so little."

"It's a bad habit of mine. I eat too little and drink too much."

"I don't mean to lecture you. You understand that, don't you?"

"Yes, I understand. You only mean to be kind. You are thinking of my welfare."

"Will you have a dessert?"

"I couldn't. Really I couldn't."

"Some coffee, at least?"

"Well, all right. A cup of coffee."

After a while the waitress came back and took the order for coffee, and a boy with a cart came and cleared the table. Avery sat erect and stared across the room, his attention caught by someone behind Lisa. She was still feeling remorse for her behavior regarding the second martini, and she had a strong compulsion to be especially friendly with him in order to make up for it.

"Do you see someone you know?" she said.

"Yes. That elderly couple over there. You can't see them from your position, of course. Their name is Chalmers. As a matter of fact, they're very old friends of the family. They used to come to the house quite frequently years ago, but recently they scarcely get out at all. I suppose I had better go speak to them. They've certainly seen me and will be expecting it. Would you like to come?"

"Is it necessary?"

"I think it would be nice if you would, but it isn't necessary, of course."

"If it isn't necessary, I won't go."

"All right. I'll make some kind of explanation. Do you object to my leaving you for a few minutes?"

"Not at all."

"Excuse me, then."

"Certainly."

He got up and walked past her and out of her range of vision, and she thought with a renewal of remorse that her compulsion toward friendliness and compatibility had not been very strong if it could not compel, so slight a concession as the exchange for his sake of a few inanities with an elderly couple. The coffee was brought and left, and she sat looking into hers but not drinking it. Minutes passed and the coffee cooled and Avery did not return. He was being delayed, it seemed, for quite a time by the elderly couple named Chalmers who were old friends of his family and who were probably garrulous and tenacious and given to exercising the prerogatives of old family friends, among which is the earned prerogative to be a bore. She was really becoming impossibly irritable, she thought, which was not good and could be corrected by a third martini, and she wished that Avery would come back and arrange it. Looking up through the archway into the bar, she saw that Emerson Page, the nice guy who did things, was sitting at the bar doing something, and what he was doing was having a drink for himself. She saw also that the stool on his right was empty, and it occurred to her that she had a perfect right to go in and occupy the stool and arrange for herself what Avery would not come and arrange. It would be quite easy to arrange in such a place of vantage, because everything was available, including a bald bartender who could be seen functioning. Getting up, she went in and occupied the stool.

"Hello, Mrs. Lawes," Emerson said. "Decide to come in where it's handy?"

"Yes. Avery is talking with someone, and it looks like going on for quite a while, so I thought I would have a martini. A third martini, to be exact."

The bartender came along, and Emerson laughed and said, "A third martini, Roscoe."

Roscoe made the martini and poured it and left on business. Lisa leaned forward on her stool and put both elbows on the bar and lifted the fragile glass in both hands.

"Your martinis are very good," she said.

He smiled. "If you like martinis. Most women seem to. My wife Ed drinks them almost exclusively. Usually I drink bourbon myself. Did you have a good time in Mexico City?"

"No," she said. "I had a perfectly horrible time in Mexico City."

Which was, she thought, what came of third martinis. On an empty stomach, anyhow. You said things that you meant but had not meant to say. You were truthful, in short, and this was dangerous and should be avoided. Since the truth was out, however, and could not be retracted, there was probably nothing imperiled in having a fourth martini, which could be had just as soon as this one was finished. She finished it and pushed the empty glass away from her on the bar with the idea that Roscoe would soon notice it and fill it.

"Why do you call her Ed?" she asked.

"What?"

"Your wife. You called her Ed. Why?"

"Her real name is Edwina. I just call her Ed for short."

"Oh. The affectionate diminutive. Is she pretty? Avery said almost everyone thinks she is."

"Well, I think so, of course. I don't know about almost everyone, however. She'll be down pretty soon, and you can judge for yourself."

"I can hardly wait," she said.

And there, she thought wearily, you go again. You are really quite impossible. All that is required is to be compatible and pleasant and to say the right things at the right time, and this is what you want to do and arc: resolved sincerely to do, but every time you open your mouth, here are these words with the most sarcastic sound, and the reason for it is that you are a coward and are afraid of these people and of what they may do to you. You are anticipating the hurt that you feel they will surely do you sooner or later, and you are therefore trying to hurt them first, including Avery, as was evident at the table, in whatever little way is available to you. Is this logical? Is this actually the reason? Well, if it is not logical, it is at least very good rationalization, and I am quite clever to think of it, and here at last is this ridiculous bartender named Roscoe to fill my glass with the fourth martini, and so it no longer matters in the least.

She lifted the full glass and also her eyes and saw Avery approaching her in the mirror. He stopped behind her and said, "Oh, here you are."

"Yes," she said. "Here I am."

He nodded to Emerson. "Been getting acquainted with Lisa, Em? Hello, Roscoe. Scotch for me. You know how."

"Right, Mr. Lawes. On the rocks."

Emerson stood up and said, "Here, Avery. Take this stool."

"No. Not at all. You keep it."

"Oh, come on. The guest always sits. That way he stays longer and drinks more."

"Well, if you put it that way."

Avery got on the stool and picked up the Scotch that Roscoe had poured.

"Did you have an interesting conversation with the old family friends?" Lisa said.

"Not very interesting, I'm afraid. I'm sorry it took so long."

"It did, didn't it? Take a long time. It took so long, in fact, that I decided to come in here and arrange for a third martini."

"Good. I'm glad you did."

"That's not all, however. I am now drinking my fourth, martini, which is one more than the third, and this will give you an idea of just how long it took."

"It's difficult to get away from an old couple like that." Avery twisted on the stool and looked over his shoulder at Emerson. "How did things go in Corinth this winter, Em?"

"Oh, fine. Everything as usual. Not as exciting as the places you've been, I guess."

"I don't know about that, Em. They're really not what they're blown up to be."

"That is right," Lisa said. "That is quite right."

She smiled and lifted her martini. Avery did not smile and lifted his Scotch. Behind them, Ed came through the archway. Emerson saw her in the mirror and turned to meet her. She was wearing a very pale blue dress that left her shoulders out, and her shoulders, he thought, were something to make you want to know what the lest of her would be like out, which was something he already knew and was happy about. Watching her approach, he felt fiercely possessive and almost exultant. "Hello, honey. I was hoping you'd come."

"Did you doubt it? Darling, I've been drooling over the thought of one of Roscoe's martinis for an hour."

"Good. You can have one with Mrs. Avery Lawes. Mrs. Lawes, this is my wife."

Lisa revolved on her stool, and Avery vacated his, stepping back beside Emerson.

"Call me Lisa," Lisa said.

"Thank you. My name is Edwina."

"Your husband says he calls you Ed. Why does he call you that?"

"Because he thinks it's cute, I think."

"Really? He told me it was only because it's short."

"Isn't that just like a man? He tells every woman something different."

"I called a girl Al once. Everyone else called her Alison, but I called her Al. I was the only one who did it. It was my special name for her."

Which was really an insane thing to say, a perverse expression of sudden pain that left her poised perilously on a razor's edge between a chasm behind and a chasm before, and she looked into the glass that had held the fourth martini and wondered why, why, why. Why did she deliberately jeopardize herself, and why did she put her fingers around her own heart, and why did she now feel in an instant, with the appearance of Ed, the intolerable and destructive way she felt? She revolved again on the stool, facing the bar, and Ed got onto the stool beside her, and Roscoe came along with the soft look on his face that was the look he kept for Ed and no one else.

"Martini, Ed?"

"Dry, Roscoe. Very dry."

"Do you have to tell me? I know just how you like them."

He fixed it that way and pushed it across to her. From the same shaker he poured the fifth that Lisa was obviously ready for and expecting.

"Avery said everyone thinks you're pretty," Lisa said. "Your husband said he doesn't know about everyone, but he thinks you are, anyhow, and I think you are too. I think you're very pretty."

"Thank you," Ed said. "You are too, you know."

"Oh, nonsense. You're just saying that. I'm much too thin and pale. Don't you think so, Avery? Don't you think I'm much too thin and pale?"

He laughed. "I think you're much too full of gin, if you want to know the truth. I think maybe we'd better be going home."

"I don't want to go home. Things are only now becoming interesting. I want to sit right here where this talented bartender can arrange martinis for me. You are lucky to have such a bartender, Mr. Page. He arranges martinis better than any bartender I have ever known."

"All right. If you want to stay, all right. But I wish that you would come home."

She looked up into the mirror, at his face in the mirror, and then she drained her glass and slipped off the stool and was at the end of the movement somehow small and contrite and all at once exceedingly tired.

"You are quite right," she said. "It is certainly time to go home."

Without saying good-night, she turned and walked through the archway into the dining room and back to the small room at the entrance where they had left their wraps, and she waited there for Avery to come, understanding that he was being polite to the Pages and saying the good-night that she had failed to say, or had deliberately refused to say through perversity, and she thought that Emerson Page, the nice guy, was someone she would probably hate more than she had ever hated anyone before.

Avery came and got their wraps, and they went outside and got into the black Caddy. She sat beside him in the front seat and leaned her head back and closed her eyes.

"I'm sorry," she said. "Truly I'm sorry."

"For what?"

"For being a perverse, nasty, unnatural bitch."

"All of that? Just because you drank too many martinis? Don't be silly, Lisa. I've been known to drink too much in Em's bar myself. It was the night before I left for Miami last November. Did I tell you about that?" It was apparent that he was going to pass it off lightly, as of no consequence, and this was probably out of kindness, which was the last thing she wanted at the moment, to be treated with kindness, and she would have preferred to have him strike her in the face.

"No," she said. "You didn't tell me."

She kept her head back and her eyes closed, and he began to tell her about it, and she sat there feeling the destructive thing that had started, and thinking that the prognosis of all this with Avery was now hopeless if it had ever been anything else and that she had better run away at once, tomorrow if not tonight, and knowing in spite of this that she would not run.

SECTION 3

Ed came out of the bathroom in nothing.

"What was the matter with her?" she said.

Emerson, in red-and-white-striped pajamas, was sitting up in bed with his back against the headboard. He looked at Ed and kept on looking at her.

"With whom?"

"You know whom. Lisa Lawes."

"She drank too many martinis."

"I know that. But why?"

"Lots of people drink too many martinis. Especially Roscoe's martinis. Roscoe's martinis, I understand, are considered exceptionally tempting."

"Don't try to high-brow talk me, you low-brow. It won't work."

"I'm not a low-brow. I'm a middle-brow. Most of the time, anyhow. The only time I'm a low-brow is when you corrupt me."

"Personally, I find you much more acceptable as a low-brow. However, that's neither here nor there when it comes to Lisa Lawes and the martinis. You know what I mean."

"Do I?"

"Certainly. Some people drink to be sociable, and some people drink for pleasure, and some people drink for other reasons of their own which are personal and usually not pleasant. That's the way it was with her. With Lisa."

"And you accused me of high-brow talking you. Honey, you're positively intellectual."

"You needn't be sarcastic, Em."

"Who's being sarcastic? I'm honestly impressed. Well, go ahead. Diagnose her for me. Tell me why Lisa drank too many martinis."

"To escape, naturally."

"Escape what?"

"How the hell would I know? Whatever she has inside her that needs escaping from. You saw how she went about it, Em. You can always tell that kind of drinker. There's a sort of deadly purpose in them."

"Is that really you saying all those things? You sound like a psychiatrist or something. Which gives me a good idea of how we could get rich fast. You could open an office and conduct all your sessions just the way you are now. For men only, of course. You'd be sensationally successful. No other psychiatrist in the world could touch you when it came to establishing rapport with the patient. Did you hear that? Rapport, I said. Don't get the idea you're the only one who knows any words."

"You're making fun of me. You aren't taking me seriously at all."

"On the contrary, I'm taking you very seriously, and I couldn't agree with you more. It's just that I don't consider the diagnosis of Lisa Lawes particularly interesting."

"Don't you?"

Ed walked over and sat down on the edge of the bed and looked pensive. Besides looking other ways. Emerson's attention was given mostly to the other ways.

"Not as interesting as you, anyhow," he said. "Not nearly as interesting."

"That's because you're not sensitive to subtleties. You respond only to the most obvious stimuli. As for me, I find her extremely interesting. Do you know why? Because she's vulnerable, and vulnerable people are always interesting. You keep wondering what their particular vulnerability is."

"Vulnerable? Vulnerable, for God's sake?"

"Yes, vulnerable. And don't sound so damned outraged about it, because it's true. You heard the thing; she said. Bitter little remarks that were intended to hurt, and she said them as if she *had* to say them, as if she couldn't *help* saying them in spite of not really wanting to. People who hurt others like that for no apparent reason are people who are afraid of being hurt themselves, and they are afraid of being hurt because they are somehow vulnerable. They anticipate the hurt to themselves and try to get in a few cracks first. What it amounts to is a kind of premature reprisal."

"Honey, you've been reading books again. Which one did you get that from?"

"I didn't get it from any books, damn it. You just don't give me credit for having any brains of my own."

"Of course I do. I not only give you credit for having brains but also for much other superior property, absolutely all of which is now on display."

"Never mind that, now. Just stay where you are. What did she say at the bar before I got there?"

"Nothing much. I asked her if she had a good time in Mexico City, and she said no, she had a perfectly horrible time."

"You call that nothing much? A brand new wife saying something like that? I consider it very significant."

"So do I, to tell the truth. I also consider it none of my damn business."

"Don't be stuffy, Em. We're not harming anyone just by discussing it between ourselves. What was it you said Avery told you that night? You remember. About not liking women."

"Oh, oh. I thought you'd get around to that."

"You did, did you? Which means we've both been thinking the same thing. Do you suppose that's why it's gone sour already?"

"You've lost me, honey. What's gone sour?"

"Damn it, Em, don't be deliberately obtuse. You know perfectly well what I mean. Their marriage, of course."

"Has it gone sour?"

"You're probably the most irritating man I've ever been married to. You were there at the bar tonight, weren't you?"

"Sure, I was there. I was there and heard too many martinis talking. You ever listened to too many martinis? They say the most peculiar things."

"Oh, to hell with you, Em Page. Be as evasive as you like. Furthermore, since you obviously want to be left alone, I think I'll just go out and sleep on the sofa."

"All right, all right. Wait a minute, woman. So I've got the same idea you've got. So the guy's impotent or something. So he got down there in Miami and met this gal and began to think he could beat it. So he found out he couldn't. After it was too late. So the gal's hungry. So she's starving, and she's about to start prowling if she hasn't already. So I've come clean with everything in my dark little mind. Satisfied?"

"Your mind's not dark. It's only little. What happens if she starts prowling around Emerson Page?"

"Worried, honey?"

"Not much. I think I can still take care of my own, which I may shortly demonstrate, just possibly. Why do I dislike her so much, Em? I thought I was a reasonably warm-hearted and generous person. It isn't like me to dislike anyone so intensely in so little time, even someone so deliberately unpleasant."

"Every married woman dislikes a woman she thinks is on the prowl, or about to go on the prowl."

"Hear the sage of Corinth. Wisdom in a capsule. Seriously, though, I guess it isn't exactly that I dislike her. It's more than that, really. She makes me crawl."

"Crawl! For God's sake, how many martinis did *you* have?"

"Just two, and I can carry four with difficulty. Not all of me, of course. Crawls, I mean. Just my flesh. On my bones, sort of. You know how it is when you see something that's repugnant to you. And I can't understand because I can't see any reason for it. She's very attractive, really, in a pale sort of way. It disturbs me."

"Look, honey. While you're crawling, why don't you just crawl into bed? Not just your flesh. All of you. Bones and all."

"Yes. I guess I'd better."

Ed sighed and stood up and stretched. She put on her nightgown, which had been lying across the bed, and instead of being in nothing she was in something that was just a little more than nothing and somehow gave the appearance of being just a little less. Emerson watched the accomplishment of this delightful paradox with curiosity and pleasure.

CHAPTER V

SECTION 1

Spring ran into summer, and summer ran into August, and August was hot. It was reported to be the hottest August on record, and in the heat of its still, white days the aberrant hunger survived and grew and became a malignant torment, and what gave it strength and made it worse was that it had ceased to be diffuse and unattached and had become directed and dedicated. During the ascent of the year and now in the early decline, Lisa continued to tell herself, as she had told herself immediately in the car returning from the restaurant, that she would have to run, that the peril involved in fidelity for the promised year was far too great, and that flight, if not the attainment of security, was at least the postponement of disaster. But she did not run. She stayed. She stayed on into the still, hot month in the precarious fulfillment of the promised year, and where she stayed precisely for a great part of the time was in Emerson Page's bar.

She was in the bar now, and it was cool and shadowy, and there were at hand the ingredients of the lift that had become more essential to existence and more difficult to gauge and sustain than ever before. She came here for a part of almost every afternoon, and this was something that she had promised herself to stop. Once she did stop for nearly a week, but then she resumed her visits and later her promises, and this running, losing fight between resolution and weakness only added to her burden of guilt and the magnitude of her despair. The real reason she came, and continued to come in spite of her promises, was not, of course, merely to gel a few drinks, which could have been had at home or elsewhere, nor to sit out of the heat in a cool and pleasant place, for there were other available places both cool and pleasant. She came to see Emerson Page, who had been blessed by contact and had become a symbol. Through him there was vicarious release, a transient abatement of hunger and pain. He was, in effect, a secondary stimulus to which she responded partially, though not fully, as to the primary.

At this time, however, he was not present, and she wanted him to be, and she was very annoyed that he was not. It seemed to her that his absence might very well be calculated to deny her deliberately her vicarious contact, and this was certainly sufficient to justify annoyance, or even anger. It was quite likely, moreover, that he had been counseled in his perversity by a shrewder and more vindictive head, and it was her conviction, after considering it, that this head was surely the bald one moving around behind the bar at this very moment. She was well aware that Roscoe did not like her and wished that she would not come here any more. Though it was antipathy unstated, it was perfectly apparent in the shades of gesture and expression, and it was all right with her, as far as that went, because she did not like him any better than he liked her, which was not at all, and as a matter of fact she considered him a repulsive oil man absolutely. She had already drunk too much and passed the stage of compatibility, and she watched him with cold distrust as he filled her glass from a shaker.

"Where's Emerson?" she said.

She had started using the Christian name quite a long time ago, right after she had begun coming in alone, and this was a mild excitement in her secret intimacy with the substance through the shadow. There was also a secondary pleasure in the use of the name in that it disturbed Roscoe, who unperceptively thought that Emerson himself was the object of her interest, and this was such a screamingly funny joke as the old fool would never understand.

"He isn't here," the old fool said.

"I can see that, of course. I can see perfectly well where he isn't. What I want to know is where he is."

"He's upstairs."

"In the apartment?"

"That's right."

"Isn't that unusual?"

"What's unusual about a man's being upstairs in his own apartment?"

"Why do you persist in asking questions of your own instead of answering mine? If you want to know what I think, I think it is no way to treat a customer."

"I'm sorry, Mrs. Lawes."

"To me it seems very strange that he should be upstairs in his apartment at this particular time. It seems very strange indeed."

"All right, Mrs. Lawes. It's strange."

"Yes, it is. It's certainly strange. What I would like to know is, what is he doing up there?"

"Well, I wouldn't know about that."

"Are you sure? Are you quite sure that you wouldn't know about that?"

"Look, Mrs. Lawes. A man goes upstairs to his apartment. Why he goes or what he does there is something I don't know anything about, and it's something I don't want to know anything about. If you want to know the truth of it, it's something I don't figure is any of my business."

"Are you being impertinent, Roscoe?"

"I hope not, Mrs. Lawes."

"Why do you continually call me Mrs. Lawes? I wish you would not continually call me Mrs. Lawes."

"What would you like me to call you?"

"Oh, never mind. I can see that it is quite futile to talk about it. Perhaps you can at least tell me when he will come downstairs."

"I'd tell you if I knew, Mrs. Lawes, but I don't."

"Doesn't he usually come down about the same time?"

"You never can tell. Sometimes he comes down one time, sometimes another. There's no way to tell."

"Do you know what it seems like to me? It seems like he may be deliberately avoiding me."

"That isn't true, Mrs. Lawes. You know better than that. Why should he avoid you?"

"That's the question, isn't it? Perhaps you could answer that one yourself."

"I told you he isn't trying to avoid you at all."

"It seems very strange, that's all." She lifted her glass and looked at him over the edge of it. "Shall I tell you something, Roscoe?"

"If you like."

"You don't like me, Roscoe."

"I wouldn't say that, Mrs. Lawes."

"I know you wouldn't say it. You wouldn't say it because you are a gentleman, and a gentleman doesn't tell a lady he doesn't like her, and besides, it would be bad for business. I would judge that I give this bar about as much business as any other person in town. Isn't that so?"

"You're a good customer, Mrs. Lawes."

She thought this was very funny, one of these classic, understatement kinds of joke, and she lowered her glass, and looked down into it and laughed for a while silently with a slight shaking of her shoulders.

"Yes. A good customer. I am quite a good customer indeed. Shall I tell you something else, Roscoe? Would you be shocked if I were quite honest with you?"

"I don't think so."

"The truth is, I don't like you, either, Roscoe. I don't like you a damn bit more than you like me. Does that disturb you?"

"It's always better if people like you, but sometimes it can't be helped if they don't."

"You're a philosopher, Roscoe. You are a philosophical bartender. Emerson told me once that you used to read poetry to him. Is that true?"

"Em talks too much."

"It's true, then. It's true, and it embarrasses you. Why are people who read poetry so often embarrassed by the fact that they read poetry?"

"I'm not embarrassed, Mrs. Lawes."

"Oh, well, deny it if it is any comfort to you. It's beside the point, anyhow. The point is, you and I don't like each other. There may be more in this than lies on the surface, Roscoe, but whatever lies below the surface, we will leave there. Is that agreed? If so, I will tell you the obvious reasons why we don't like each other. To begin, you don't like me because you are a kind of self-appointed guardian of Emerson Page and Ed Page, who are your own precious pair, and it is your opinion that I am a predatory female on the prowl, and that Emerson is the one I am currently on the prowl for, and that he is the kind of guy who, in favorable circumstances, could definitely be had. This is the reason you don't like me, Roscoe, and the reason I don't like you is that you are a fool, and just why you are a fool, and just how big a fool you are, I will not say, because this is my secret and amuses me very much. What do you say to all this? Am I right?"

"I don't think we ought to be talking this way, Mrs. Lawes."

"Don't you? Do you think it's improper? Do you think I am an improper woman?"

"I didn't suggest that, Mrs. Lawes."

"On the contrary, you did suggest it. You very definitely suggested it. However, I am not at all offended, so we had just as well drop it. I will only repeat that what you think is very amusing. It would be even more amusing if you were capable of seeing just how amusing it is."

"I'm glad I amuse you, Mrs. Lawes. I guess it's part of my job. Now you will have to excuse me. I have a customer."

"Certainly, Roscoe. You are certainly excused."

He went off to his customer, and she was no longer amused. She was depressed and frightened, and she told herself that she would finish her drink and go away and not return to this place again, ever again, but she knew quite well that she would return nevertheless, just as she always did, because here was the secondary source of desire, and here, in truth, was the primary source also, but the primary source was strictly forbidden and heavy with peril and was susceptible only to vicarious attainment through the secondary.

I will go away, she thought, *I will go away*, and knew that she would not.

And so she continued to sit, and eventually had another drink, and in time Emerson Page came in behind the bar and stood across from her in the borrowed significance of which he did not dream.

"Hello, Mrs. Lawes," he said.

I will be quite casual, she thought. *I will be merely a lady who has stopped in for a drink in the most natural way.*

And she looked at him and felt the stirring of her early hatred and subsequent concession, a reaction of conflict that resulted from his being in her mind both an interloper and a medium, and she was not casual in the least.

"Where have you been?" she said.

"Upstairs in the apartment, taking a break. I was out earlier, and it pooped me. Hot. I've never seen it so hot around here. Hundred and ten at three o'clock, I understand."

"Was Ed with you?"

"Ed? Not much. You couldn't drag her out of that air-conditioned apartment on a day like this."

"I didn't mean was she out with you earlier. I meant in the apartment."

"Oh. Yes. She was with me. Still there. Did you want to see her, Mrs. Lawes?"

"Why do you call me Mrs. Lawes? Why don't you call me Lisa?"

"Lisa, I mean."

"I've told you and told you to call me Lisa. Perhaps it's significant that you always call me Mrs. Lawes. Maybe it's a kind of unconscious sign that you don't like me."

"Oh, come off it, Lisa. Of course I like you."

"I'm not so sure. Roscoe doesn't like me, and Ed doesn't like me, and it's quite possible that you don't like me, either."

"Whatever gave you the idea that Ed doesn't like you?"

"I have a feeling about such things. It's practically infallible. I can always tell."

"Well, this is one time your practically infallible feeling is all wrong. Ed likes you very much."

"Really?"

"Certainly."

"You're not just telling me that?"

"Of course not."

"Then why doesn't she ever come to see me? Why doesn't she ever invite me to come to see her? The only time we ever meet is when we happen to be here at the same time, or accidentally somewhere."

"Well, to be frank about it, Lisa, the Laweses and the Pages have just never moved in the same social circle. I guess Ed would naturally be pretty shy about trying to move in. She'd be afraid someone would get the wrong idea about it."

"That's silly. That's perfectly silly. Avery likes you. He likes you better than anyone else."

"I don't know about that, but, anyhow, it isn't the point."

"No? Can you tell me just what is the point?"

"I'm afraid not. It's pretty confusing to a simple guy like me. I don't know exactly what the point is, but I know what it isn't, and it sure as hell isn't just whether or not you happen to like a guy."

"You know what I think? I think you're only rationalizing. You have a feeling of inferiority and are trying to convince yourself that it's something else."

He laughed. "All right. Maybe that's it."

"Not that it matters, because you are obviously not telling me the truth, anyhow. The truth is, both you and Ed dislike me and don't want to have any more to do with me than is necessary."

"You don't really believe that."

"Do you think I am lying?"

"Oh, for Christ's sake, Lisa! Listen to me. Ed and I both like you. We like you very much, and that's all there is to it."

"Well, in your case I may be open to conviction, but in Ed's, I'm certain I am right."

"No, you're not. You're absolutely wrong."

She picked up her glass and saw that it was empty and set it down and pushed it toward him.

"Then we had better have a drink together."

"Are you sure you want another?"

"Quite sure. You needn't worry about it. I'm used to drinking a great deal."

"I know."

"What do you mean, you know?"

"Nothing, Lisa. It was just a remark."

"To me it had an unpleasant sound. As if it meant something."

"Wrong again. It doesn't mean a thing."

He fixed drinks for them. He would have made hers light, but he knew very well that she would have realized it immediately and made an issue of it, so he stuck to the prescribed ratio. She tasted it and was satisfied.

"She's very lovely," she said.

"What?"

"Ed. She's very lovely."

"Oh. Yes, she is, isn't she?"

"How long have you been married?"

"Ten years. A little longer."

"Ten years is a long time."

"Not with Ed. Not nearly long enough."

She thought of the things that had happened to her in the last decade, and it seemed like a very long time indeed. A long, bitter time. She wondered what kind of life it would be that could make ten years seem short. "A lot can happen in ten years," she said.

"That's right. In ten years Ed and I have come from a cheap short-order place to this. I don't mean it's so much, after all, but it has made money for us, and it has made us happy. It's what we wanted, and it's what we got."

"Some people are lucky to get what they want."

"Sure they are. And you're one of them. It seems to me that you've been a hell of a lot luckier than most."

"Does it? Well, it would be quite futile to try to convince you otherwise, I can see that. Besides, it makes absolutely no difference what you believe, so it is unnecessary to try. Do you still love her?"

Emerson looked at her for a moment with a stricken look in his face, as if the sudden, brutal inference that he might *not* love Ed left him mute and isolated in a terrible emptiness. After a moment he laughed at the incredible idea.

"Excuse me for laughing, Lisa. It's just that I find the idea of not loving Ed completely unbelievable."

"Why are you so sure? I don't mean love her the way they say it gets after you've been married for a long time. You know the way I don't mean. A dull kind of business of mutual respect and devotion to servitude with an occasional tepid concession *to* love. I mean, do you still want her and hunger for her with passion?"

He was a guy with practically no false modesty, and he was rarely embarrassed, but now he was, and he wished that she would quit talking this way. He wondered how the hell it turned out that he was always having a Lawes get intimate with him. She was looking down into her glass with fierce intensity, and he had the strange, stripped feeling that she was seeing in the pale liquid a kind of mental picture of him and Ed in bed. This he considered an invasion of privacy, and it made him angry as well as embarrassed, and he had a hard time containing his anger. He managed it only by reminding himself that she was a woman with normal needs who was married to a personable dud and that her needs must be unfulfilled. She was starving, he thought, and he was truly sorry for her.

"I love her the same as I always have," he said.

She shook her head, still staring intently into the glass.

"That's an equivocation. That is obviously an equivocation."

"Look, Lisa. I don't think you want me to give you a clinical description of Ed and me making love."

She looked up at him across the bar then, and he was shocked by what he saw in her eyes, and what he saw was hate and pain. He realized at once that she had been torturing herself deliberately by speaking as she had, and there was almost, but not quite, a flash of insight into the reason she had done this.

"What I think," she said, "is that you are a man and are incapable of loving her properly for that reason for no other. Men are by nature dull and coarse and are neither sensitive nor tender enough to love properly."

"Don't talk like that, Lisa."

"And now you are angry with me."

"No, I'm not angry. I just don't want you to talk like that about Ed and me."

She slipped off the stool and stood beside it erect and quite steady in spite of the amount she had drunk.

"Despite your denial, it is quite apparent that you are angry, and it is also quite apparent, as I said before, that you dislike me very much."

"Damn it, Lisa, do we have to go over that again?"

"If you didn't dislike me, you would come to our party. You and Ed."

"What party?"

"The one Avery is having at the country club Saturday night. It is only a small party for a few people."

"No one has asked us to come."

"I'm asking you now."

"Well, I don't know. Saturday night is a pretty busy time around here."

"You see? You just don't want to come. Already you are making excuses."

"Does Avery know you are inviting us?"

"What Avery knows or does not know is not pertinent. I have the right to invite someone to the party if I choose. The point is this: Will you come or will you not come?"

"All right, Lisa. We'll come. Thanks for asking us."

"Not at all. Eight would be a good time. Sometime around eight."

She turned and walked steadily across the room and outside into the street, and Roscoe walked down to Emerson behind the bar.

"That's a crazy woman," he said.

"She's just had too much to drink, Roscoe."

"Sure. She's always just had too much to drink. People don't drink that way for fun, Em. There's something crazy in them that makes them do it."

"She's hungry, Roscoe. She's married to a dud."

"Avery?"

"That's right. He's a dud."

"So that's why she's after you!"

"Don't be silly, Roscoe. She isn't after me."

"The hell she isn't! You just be sure she never gets you cornered, that's all."

"Don't make me laugh, Roscoe. I feel sorry for her."

"In my opinion, it's wasted sympathy. She's the most quarrelsome damn woman I ever saw."

"I told you, Roscoe. She's frustrated. Frustrated people get that way."

"Okay. I'm just a damn dumb bartender, and I don't know anything about frustrated people or the way they're supposed to get, but I know a woman on the make when I see one, and this is a woman on the make. She's a bad one, Em. I've got a feeling about her. You take an old man's advice and keep hands off."

"You shouldn't have said that, Roscoe. You know how it is with Ed and me."

"Sure, Em, I know. I guess I talk too much."

"It's all right."

Roscoe went back to work, and Emerson kept remembering Lisa's eyes, the hate and pain in them.

It was for me, he thought. *The hate was for me.*

This was something he could not understand, and it disturbed him very much. He had not intended to have a second drink so early, but he poured it and stood there drinking it.

SECTION 2

In the street, the dry and searing heat came up around Lisa from the pavement. She went directly home, but when she was there she did not go immediately into the house, but went instead around the house into the back yard and down past the old summerhouse to the edge of the bluff overlooking the river and the wide bottom land. The river below was a gray and withered vein in the blistered body of earth. Beyond the river, marking the far boundary of the bottoms, the ridge was an ugly protrusion of bone with its quondam green flesh darkened and shrunken away. She stood staring out across the river and the bottoms to the ridge, remembering her recent insanity in the bar, frightened and impaired by her perverse penchant for self-destruction, and pretty soon she lowered her eyes to the rocks and tangled brush at the foot of the bluff that fell away almost perpendicularly before her. She began to wonder what it would be like to throw herself down, and she could see quite vividly for a moment her broken body in the brush, all that was left of the hunger and hope and perversity that she had been, and she felt for herself in death a great pity. It would be a great relief to be dead, she thought, but the prospect of dying was a terrifying prospect, because dying was not a part of death but the last part of living, and if she were to throw herself down upon the rocks among the brush there would be to endure the eons of seconds in descent and final pain.

Shrinking away from the thought and the edge of the bluff, she went back a few yards to the garden swing and sat down. It was getting quite late. Sunlight had ascended the ridge beyond the river and would soon slip upward off the crest to leave the last of the visible world in a long summer's dusk, but there would be little relief in the dusk from the sun's heat, for that was held in the earth itself and its appurtenances. Even the swing on which she sat was quite hot. She could feel the narrow slats like brands across her body. The oppressive air seemed to swell and contract with the undulating sound of unseen cicadas, and she could hear behind her, approaching on the dry grass, someone moving with slow and heavy footsteps.

It was Avery. He sat down beside her and sighed and let his head rest against the back of the swing.

"It's so hot," he said. "It takes the strength out of you."

"Yes."

"Wouldn't it be more comfortable in the house?"

"I suppose it would."

"What are you doing down here?"

"As you see, I am sitting in the swing and looking across the river to the ridge."

"I used to sit here a lot when I was a kid. I would sit and watch the river and try to imagine what it was like when this was the frontier and the wagon trains were going west."

"I know. You've told me about it."

"Have I? I'm sorry if I'm repetitious. What have you been thinking about while you've been here?"

"Just before you came I was trying not to think at all, and before that I was standing at the edge of the bluff and wishing that I had the nerve to throw myself down."

"You don't mean that, Lisa."

"Don't I? All right, have it your own way. I don't mean it."

"I've tried very hard to make you satisfied."

"Oh, it isn't your fault that you've become involved in an impossible situation. I am well aware of that. It's my fault, and I am perfectly willing to acknowledge it."

"It's not your fault. So far as I can see, there is no blame attached to either of us. I wish you would stop being so ready to condemn yourself."

"It must be very annoying to you."

"No. I only wish I knew why you get so depressed. Have you had a bad day?"

"Not particularly. It was neither better nor worse than most other days, which is bad enough, God knows."

"Perhaps you need more to do. Something to keep you occupied and interested."

She laughed. "You mean like occupational therapy? Thank you for being so concerned."

"You've been drinking. Have you been to Em Page's bar again?"

"Yes. I was there for quite a long time and had quite a few drinks."

"I thought you had decided not to go there alone any more."

"I did decide that. I promised myself that I wouldn't go, but now I've started going again. I'm very good at breaking promises. It's one of the things I'm best at."

"You say that as if you were proud of it."

"I'm not proud of it. It's the truth that I can't think of anything I've ever done in my life that I'm proud of. Not a single thing. It is only that I am very tired and worn out with pretending. There is a certain relief in facing things squarely. It's called catharsis, I think. I went to a psychiatrist once, and that is what he called it."

"There is also a certain relief for some people in assuming guilt that is not properly theirs. I didn't know you had gone to a psychiatrist. When was it?"

"I was in college at the time."

"Why did you go?"

"My parents sent me because I tried to kill myself, and it frightened them. I was very cowardly about it, of course. I might have done it in a way that would have been certain if I'd had the nerve, but I didn't. I only took some sleeping tablets, and it was not successful."

"It is not always unsuccessful. My mother did that, and it worked very well. She took the tablets at night and was dead in the morning."

"I was under the impression that your mother died of a heart condition."

"That's the impression that practically everyone is under, thanks to the code of the Laweses. In the code of the Laweses, unpleasant things are carefully disguised as something else. But that is irrelevant and hardly worth talking about. Why did you try to kill yourself?"

"For the same reason your mother actually did kill herself, I suppose. Because I felt that I didn't want to live any longer."

"That's hardly an answer."

"Yes, it is. It is the answer to the question you asked."

"All right. Why did you feel that you didn't want to live any longer?"

"Well, that's another question and needs another answer. I could say that I was depressed, but then you would want to know why I was depressed, and pretty soon I would have to tell you something you certainly don't want to hear."

"If we are going to make a success of our marriage, there are many things, I think, that I should hear."

"Are you still holding to the hope that we can make a success of our marriage?"

"Aren't you?"

"No. It is quite hopeless."

"Then why do you stay?"

"You know why I stay. Because I promised to try for a year, and the year is not up."

"But you are quite good at breaking promises. It's one of the things you're best at. Isn't that what you said?"

"Nevertheless; this is one that I am trying to keep. I will go away if you want me to, however. You only have to say so."

"I don't want you to go, Lisa. Our year is just over half gone. I'm still convinced that we can reach a satisfactory adjustment in time."

"You think we can learn to love each other? You honestly think that?"

"Perhaps not. Not in a physical way, at least. But there are other values."

"Spiritual values, you mean? One hears so much about them, but I'm not sure I know just what they are. I am no philosopher, you understand, but it seems to me that thought and emotion do not exist independently. They must surely have at least a physical source, and if the source is no good, if it is distorted or in some way wrong, the thought and emotion are also distorted and wrong, and that is just too bad for the person concerned."

"Do you deny the possibility of any kind of correction?"

"In my case, I deny it. Last December in Miami I honestly thought that it might be possible, and I have tried to go on thinking it, but now I am sure that it is not so."

"Have you never loved anyone at all, Lisa?"

"Are you sure you want me to answer that? I told you that I am very tired and worn out with pretending. If I answer, I will tell you the truth."

"I wish you would."

She had not looked at him since he had sat down beside her. She did not look at him now. She continued to start out across the river valley to the ridge on the other side, and the light had now left the crest, and the darkening air swelled and collapsed and swelled again with the persistent rhythm of the unseen cicadas in the listless trees.

"Very well, then," she said. "I have loved more than once with an ardor that would surprise you. In the beginning there was a girl named Alison, and it was a long time ago. It seems to me, anyhow, like a long time. She was tall and slim and strong and very good at games and things like that, and it was my opinion that she was the most wonderful person who had ever been born or was ever likely to be born. I loved her very much, and for a while she loved me too, but then she didn't love me any more, and this was because of something that happened. I wrote her a note and lost it, and someone found it, a teacher in the school we went to, and that was the end of it, of course, and it was all my fault. She said that I was careless about the note, which was true, and I didn't blame her for being angry, and I still don't blame her. No one understood about it, and we were treated like criminals, and it isn't right for someone like her to be treated that way. I would have given up everyone else for her sake, the whole world, but she said that I was a fool and that she never wanted to see me again. It wasn't quite that way, however. I did see her many times afterward, but we were like strangers, and it was far worse than not seeing her at all. Do you want me to go on?"

"I'm not sure that I understand what you are trying to tell me."

"I think you are. I think you are very sure. Later, one summer at a lake, there was someone else. It didn't amount to much. It was just something that happened in the summer and was not expected to last or to mean any more than it obviously did. After that there was no one else for quite a long time, but I was often very depressed, and it was then, sometimes during that period, that I took the barbiturates but did not die. I wanted to die, I believe I was sincere in that, but I did not want to do any of the things that would have made dying certain, and after the attempt which failed I did not try again. Eventually I was glad for a while that I hadn't succeeded in dying, however, for I was in college then, Midland

City College, and there was a teacher there who taught French. She was French herself, I believe, or had been born in France at least, and she was very sleek and sophisticated, and all the men in her class were excited about her, which was a great joke on them that they never understood. It was wonderful with her at first, as if I had been lifted to a new, exhilarating life, but it couldn't last long because of circumstances. Because of her position in the college, I mean. You can see that, of course. The perils were multiplied, and the consequences of exposure were far too severe to be risked indefinitely. I have found that nothing can survive in the shadow of a constant threat. Nothing on earth has the strength for that."

She stopped and waited and was apparently listening for some sound in the hot dusk, but actually she was only giving him time to say something or strike her or do what he felt impelled to do in the circumstances. She still did not look at him, but she knew that he had not moved and was still sitting with his head back against the swing, and she had a feeling that his eyes were closed and had been closed all the time she had been talking. After a while he repeated his long sigh.

"Is that all?" he said.

"No, it is not all, but perhaps it is enough."

"I want you to tell it all."

"All right. Just as you wish. Bella was the last. I met her in a park during a particularly bad time, and we met there two or three times afterward, and I went to live with her in her apartment. It was never very good with Bella, not like with the others, but it was better than being alone, and I stayed with her until it was no longer possible. She found out that my family had money and wanted me to help her blackmail them, and it was this that made it impossible to stay. Against my will, she contacted my brother Carl and had him come to the apartment, and he came and paid her five thousand dollars, and this was the night he took me away with him and three or four days later took me to Miami."

He stirred and sighed again and spoke so softly that she could barely hear him.

"To meet me."

"Yes. You were in bad luck. You probably won't believe it, but I'm truly sorry."

"Why did you marry me?"

"For asylum. Carl thought that marriage would eventually convert me to normalcy, that it was the only way. He had been very kind to me, and I wanted to please him. He wanted me to change, and I honestly wanted to change myself. I even convinced myself that it would be possible in the way you offered, but now I know that it is not possible and can never be accomplished. I'm sorry for the hurt I've done you."

"You needn't be. I deserve what I've received."

"What? What do you mean?"

"I had no capacity for marriage myself. I was using you as much as you were using me."

"Oh, that. That's different."

"Yes? How?"

"Impotence can be adjusted to. Even compensated for. If only that were between us, we would have no great problem. Anyhow, it will serve no purpose now to weigh the blame. You said that yourself a little while ago, and I agree with you. The only question is, what do you intend to do about it?"

"Do? What's to be done?"

"I must say you are taking it very calmly. Don't you find me disgusting? Don't you want to strike me or curse me or even kill me?"

"No."

"I don't understand it."

"Maybe I am too tired. Do you think you are the only one who has ever been tired or depressed or has wanted to die?"

His voice did not rise with emotion. It was perfectly flat and lifeless. She turned her head and looked at him for the first time since his arrival, and he was sitting as she had thought he was, with his head back and his eyes closed, and his face had in the dusk the stiff, waxen look of a face that had been embalmed.

"I told you I should go away," she said, "and now I will go."

"Break your promise?"

"I think you are now willing to relieve me of it."

"No. I am not."

"Why? Do you want me to stay so that you can punish me in some way? If you do, I will not blame you."

"I don't want to punish you. I am in no position to assume a judicial role, God knows."

"Then why do you want me to stay?"

"Because I am obligated by the fraud I practiced on you, which was as great, in spite of what you say, as the one you practiced on me. Because I cannot release you without first trying to help you. What does it matter? You have made a promise, and I will hold you to it."

"You are being kind, and I wish you wouldn't. No good has come of kindness. Carl was kind, and you can see what it has come to."

"I will take you somewhere for treatment."

"I won't go. No good has come of treatment, either. If you have faith in treatment, why haven't you sought it for yourself?"

"I don't know. At any rate, I won't try to force you to do anything you don't want to do. Do you intend to stay?"

"If you still want it."

"I do. I am trying to think why it is that I want it, and I believe it is because I am convinced that this is the last chance for both of us, and if it can't be the beginning of something better, it should at least be the end of everything bad."

"All right. If I am going to stay, I had better tell you that I invited Emerson and Ed Page to the party Saturday night."

For a moment he did not understand what she had said, his mind struggling to adjust to the incredibly quick shift of hers from their personal tragic relationship to such petty business. Actually, the shift was not so abrupt nor the new subject so unassociated as they appeared, but this was something he did not know.

"Party? Oh, yes. Em and Ed? Why did you do that?"

"Because I wanted them to come. They are the only people in Corinth I can tolerate. Do you object?"

"No. Of course not. I'm a little surprised that they accepted."

"It was he who accepted. I don't think he wanted to, but I rather tricked him into it."

"Well, they're welcome. I like Em. Perhaps he'll help to make the evening bearable." He opened his eyes and stood up slowly, as if the action required tremendous effort. "I'm going up to the house now. Are you ready to come?"

"Not yet. I want to sit here a little longer."

"Will you be all right?"

"Perfectly. If you are afraid I may throw myself off the bluff after all, you needn't be. I am really too great a coward."

Turning, he walked away. She listened to his footsteps receding on the dry grass. The valley of the river was filling with darkness.

CHAPTER VI

SECTION 1

Awakening very early in the morning, she knew at once that it was going to be a bad day. Bad days were in her life nothing unusual, of course, but some days were bad even in comparison with other days that were bad, and it had been that kind of day when she had taken the barbiturates quite a while ago, and it had been that kind of day when she had gone to the park and met Bella, and every time a day like that came along she knew that she would be far better off if she didn't have to live it. She lay quietly in bed with the still house around her and the bad day ahead of her, and pretty soon she realized that it was Saturday, the day of the party at the country club, and that, however bad the day might be, the night would certainly be worse. Lying there with her eyes closed and not moving a muscle, she tried to think of a way to avoid the bad day and the worse night, but she couldn't think of a way for the simple reason that there wasn't any, and then she thought that she would continue to lie quietly in the darkness behind her lids until she went to sleep again, thereby at least-shortening the day if not the night, but she couldn't do that, either. She opened her eyes and began waiting for whatever was going to happen to start happening.

In due time, she heard Mrs. Lamb, the housekeeper and cook, who slept out and came in early, clump across the back porch below and let herself in the back door with her own key. Later she heard the yardman working in the yard beside the house, though God knew what work there was for him to do with the grass and all the flowers seared and sapped by the relentless sun, and later still Avery came out of his room and down the hall and stopped outside her door. When he knocked softly, she twisted her head on her pillow and looked at the door but did not speak nor move in excess of the twisting of her head. She kept her eyes on the knob, waiting to see if it began to turn, and when it did begin she immediately closed her eyes and kept them closed. He came into the room and stopped a few feet from the bed and was silent for a minute before he spoke her name. She could hear him breathing and smell his shaving lotion, and she could see him in the dark and private little world behind her lids as he leaned forward slightly from the hips and peered at her to try to determine if she was waking or not. She did not answer, and he spoke again, and she still did not answer, and he went out and closed the door. Hearing his footsteps descending the stairs, she opened her eyes again and began to wonder what made some bad days so much worse than other bad days.

It is not, she thought, anything in the days themselves. Looking back on them, it is impossible to find any reason at all why these were the days when one particularly wanted to die, or to have others die, or felt that it was absolutely essential to do something to change the intolerable procession of degrading days, while at the same time one was irrationally terrified of any change whatever. No, it is not in the day but in oneself that the badness begins and grows with no discernible logic in its beginning and growing today rather than yesterday or tomorrow, and it is not a result of overt misfortune but of intangible oppression that builds and builds to the absolute certainty of proximate destruction. Therefore, since it is in oneself that it begins and grows, and since there is no logic in the beginning and growing, it follows that there is nothing to be done about it, except to bear it and get through it, and if one is lucky this is something that can be done.

She heard the yardman start the power mower and wondered why on earth he was starting the mower when there was no grass to cut. She heard Avery's Caddy go past the house in the drive and wondered if Avery would be back before evening and hoped that he wouldn't. She heard Mrs. Lamb's heavy tread on the stairs and in the hall and waited for Mrs. Lamb's heavy rapping to sound on the door. It did, and she took her time deciding whether to tell Mrs. Lamb to come in or go away or simply to ignore the rapping altogether, as she had done with Avery's. After a while she decided that it would be just as well on the whole to get Mrs. Lamb in and out and finished with as quickly as possible.

"Come in," she said.

Mrs. Lamb opened the door and stepped inside the room, leaving the door open behind her. She was a strong, blocky woman with a massive chests so tightly bound that it gave the appearance of being undivided, and Lisa had once, seeing the remarkable chest, had a joke pop into her head about it, a kind of humorous analogy with one part to be supplied, and the analogy was, what is to a woman as a dromedary is to a camel? The answer was, of course, Mrs. Lamb. There were several things wrong with the analogy, however, and as a joke it really had something wrong with it too, which was that it wasn't, after all, a very funny joke. It was impossible, anyhow, to imagine Mrs. Lamb being amused by it.

"Good-morning, Mrs. Lawes," Mrs. Lamb said.

"Good-morning, Mrs. Lamb."

"Will you have breakfast this morning?"

"No, thank you."

"You didn't have breakfast yesterday morning."

"I seldom eat breakfast."

"Nor day before yesterday morning."

"I know."

"You ought to eat breakfast. It's the most important meal of the day. When you start having children, you will wish you had eaten your breakfast."

"I consider it unlikely that I'll ever start having children, Mrs. Lamb."

Which was worse than the repudiation of a sacred function. It was dereliction of duty not to produce a Lawes, specifically a male Lawes, in an apprehensive world that was presently in the precarious position of having only one left. Mrs. Lamb was privately of the opinion that this production should have begun some months ago, and she was totally incapable of understanding how any woman could be reluctant to do the producing. She would have been almost willing to undertake it herself.

"I could bring it up in a tray," she said.

"I do not want any breakfast, Mrs. Lamb."

"Very well. Is there anything else I can do for you?"

"Yes, there is. You can go away and leave me alone." Mrs. Lamb flushed and left, slamming the door, and Lisa began immediately to wish that she hadn't said what she had, and then she began to wonder if it would be possible to remember even a fraction of the times she had said something and wished afterward that she hadn't, and she knew that it would not. Oh, Christ, what a bitch you are, she thought. What a bitch you are, and what a day it has begun to be with your very gracious treatment of this woman who wished for nothing but to be kind and to bring you your breakfast on a tray. It is quite apparent already that this is a day which should be eliminated, that it would be a good thing to skip at once to tomorrow, but it is also quite apparent that the only way to eliminate a day is to live it, so there is nothing to be done, and after the day is the night, and what in Christ's name is to be done with the night?

She was beginning to feel uncomfortable, and so she got out of bed and went into the bathroom and then returned and lay down on the bed again and began to think of those she had known, of Alison and Bella and others, who were no longer threats in themselves but were symbols of the threat that survived them. This was not good, was part of the bad day getting worse, and she tried thinking of Carl, how remarkably kind he was, and of Avery, how even more remarkably kind he was, and she wished to God they would quit crucifying her with their cursed kindness, and this wish made her feel guilty and debased and contributed more to the bad day getting worse than Alison and Bella and the others. Trying to achieve a kind of neutrality in her thinking, she considered the party at the country club, but this was no help because the party was assuming the proportions of a terrifying ordeal. And that, of course, was the clue to the bad day. When the past is a depressant and the future is a threat, the bad day is a trap between them, and there is no escape unless you can find it in a bottle.

Thinking of a drink, she began to want one badly, but it would never do to drink today because of tonight, which had to be gotten through somehow and would be difficult enough at best and could be survived only by drinking just ahead of time and just enough to establish and secure the lift that was her only protection. There had been other times when she had resolved not to drink, either for some specific reason or just because she was convinced that drinking was bad for her and should be stopped, and she had then tried substituting coffee for alcohol on the grounds that it was easier to do without something if you immediately put something else in its place instead of leaving an emptiness where it had been. Every time she had wanted a drink and was in danger of submitting, she had made or bought a cup of coffee and drunk it, but eventually she had given up this technique simply because it was impossible for anyone to go on drinking *that* much coffee indefinitely. Now, however, though it had never worked before, she decided that she would try it again, just for this one day, and she got off the bed and put on slippers and a robe and went downstairs to the kitchen.

It was very hot in the kitchen, because it was not air-conditioned like some of the rooms in the house. She found the glass pot of coffee that had been left over from Avery's breakfast and put it on the stove and switched on the electricity and sat down to wait in a straight chair by the table. She could hear Mrs. Lamb vacuuming in the front part of the house. The power mower started up again outside and ran a little while and died, and she decided that the yardman was adjusting the motor or something, and that was why he was running it even though there was no grass to cut. It was really extremely hot. A still, oppressive heat in which you could hear, if you listened intently, a whisper of menacing movement. Perspiration gathered in her armpits and trickled down over her ribs. Strangely, the perspiration felt icy cold. She listened to the menacing whisper in the still heat and was suddenly aware that she was about to scream. She closed her throat abruptly upon the scream, and it died with a whimper in a spasm of pain. Getting up, she went to the cabinet where the china was kept and got a cup and carried it to the stove. She poured coffee into the cup and returned with it to her chair at the table. Sitting with her elbows on the table and her head supported by her hands, she stared down into the black liquid and knew that it wasn't going to work this time either, the technique of substitution, and that she was certainly going to have a drink in spite of all tricks and resolutions. Once this truth was accepted, it was only reasonable to believe that the drink had as well come now as later. Leaving the coffee untasted in its cup on the table, she went into the hall and down the hall to the library, where there was a liquor cabinet. She got a bottle and a glass from the cabinet and carried them upstairs to her room.

Just one, she thought. Just one small drink will be quite sufficient, and there will be no need for another until tonight, when drinking will be expected and acceptable.

She poured the drink and drank it and lay down again on the bed and began to think about the party at the country club that night. It was going to be only a small party with a few people there to whom Avery thought he was obligated for one thing or another, and she had safely gotten through several more formidable affairs since she had come to Corinth, and there was actually no reason at all why it should be dreaded so excessively. She lay there and told herself this, but it did no good, and no matter how she diagnosed the situation or tried to see it for the small matter that it should have been, she understood that the party was some-how established in a pattern of peril, the consummation of the bad day that had started with waking, and that it should., if possible, be avoided at any cost. This was at first a feeling, but it was soon a conviction, and avoidance of the party was essential to survival. She started scheming how this could best be accomplished, and she came to the conclusion af-ter quite a while that she would simply say that she was too ill to go. This would not be, anyhow, an absolute lie, for she was really not feeling at all well. She had slept poorly in the night, and there was a terrible pressure inside her skull. What she needed, she thought, was to go back to sleep, and if she had another small drink she might possibly be able to do it.

She had it and began to think about Ed Page, who had been there waiting to be thought about all the time but had been resisted up to this point. Now she thought about Ed deliberately in all the ways she had thought about her over and over again, and this was a mistake, as she very well knew, for Ed was the siren of a shining, deadly island, the symbol of a particular ruin. In the torment of thinking, however, there was at least a kind of release from depression, the insubstantial peace of submission. Inviting Eel and Emerson to the party at the club had been a suicidal thing to do, exceeding even her usual proclivity for do-ing suicidal things, and she had alternated afterward between excitement and dread, and finally had refused to think about it at all. But now it was different. Now there was nothing to be lost in thinking about it, because she was herself not going to the party, and it no longer mattered. She lay and thought, and in the uneasy peace thus established, because she was exhausted, she eventually went back to sleep.

She awoke in the middle of the afternoon with the feeling that she had been on the brink of disaster and had awakened just in time, not to avoid it, but to delay it. Her heart was beating hard and fast, and she lay and listened to its beating, feeling the force of it against her ribs. Danger had slipped with her from the sleeping to the waking world and was hovering with infinite patience in the silent room. She got up abruptly and the room, with the motion, became violently alive, its parts merging and spinning and absorbing in an instant all the light of the world. She sat down on the edge of the bed in darkness until the dizziness passed, and she remembered that she had eaten nothing all day and would certainly have to take something into her stomach soon, even though the thought of it made her feel faintly nauseated. Mrs. Lamb was surely gone, because she worked only a half day on Saturdays, but perhaps she had prepared a cold lunch of some kind before she left. If so, it would be in the refrigerator, and she decided that she would go down and see, but first she would have a shower and get dressed.

She removed her robe and gown and stood looking at herself in the full length mirror of her dressing table. It was very strange how she felt about her own body, fiercely possessive with a kind of wild and terrible sadness, as if it were something apart that had been assigned to her custody for the care and protection she could not provide. It was like a child, her own child, and she had somehow failed it. Sometimes, looking at it, she would stroke it and croon to it and feel like crying because it was not stronger and lovelier and more like other bodies she had known. But now she saw it and felt only despair and wished never to see it again. Going into the bathroom, she had the shower and then returned a few minutes later to the bedroom and covered the body with clothing without looking at it again, except partially and quickly as was necessary in dressing.

In the hall below, she stood at the foot of the stairs and wondered what it was she had come down for. She had come for a specific reason, she remembered, but she could not remember what it was, and now that the dizziness had passed and she had been a little revived by the shower, she had completely forgotten about not having eaten and the necessity for food. She was only aware that whatever had followed her from sleeping to waking had also followed her from the bedroom to here and would follow her wherever she went in the house, and that it was therefore necessary to get out of the house at once. She went out the front door and around the house into the back yard and down all the way to the swing near the edge of the bluff overlooking the river valley. A few nights ago, she recalled, she had sat here and told Avery the truth about herself. There had been a kind of satisfaction in it at the time, but it had not come to anything, apparently, and in fact nothing had been said about it since, and she suspected that this was another example of his God-damn depressing kindness that was always placing her under some sort of moral obligation. The yardman, she noticed, was no place to be seen or heard. No doubt he had found it too hot to work, and it was indeed excessively hot. It was dry and blistering heat, destructive heat, the kind that could easily kill you if you weren't careful. It was, as a matter of fact, far too hot to be sitting in the swing, it was already getting unbearable, and the only thing to do was to go back into the house in spite of whatever was waiting there. In the house she could probably find some gin and soda and lemon juice and make a tall Tom Collins and drink it slowly in the living room, which was air-conditioned. In this way, it would be possible to wear out the time until Avery came home to take her to the party she wasn't going to, and maybe tomorrow would be a better day, but this was hardly likely.

She got up and went back into the house and found the ingredients for the Tom Collins and made it. In the living room, she sat in a large chair and looked out through a window into the bright still day and sipped the cold drink slowly, and by sitting quietly and thinking as little as possible she was able to induce a kind of semi-trance through which the remainder of the afternoon slipped silently in an illusion of peace. The only time she moved from the chair was when she became aware that her glass was empty and got up to fill it. She returned at once and was still there when the light outside had lost its brightness and Avery came home.

He came into the living room and said, "Hello, Lisa."

"Hello," she said.

"How was your day?"

"Rotten. My day was rotten."

"I'm sorry to hear it."

"Please don't be sorry. I'm sick of people being sorry about things."

"Perhaps the party will cheer you up. You need to get out more."

"Do I? Is that what I need? It's very comforting to know that there is someone around who knows immediately just exactly what it is that I need."

"I don't want to quarrel with you, Lisa. Are you drinking a Tom Collins?"

"Yes. That's what it is. It's my second one, and earlier I had two straight whiskeys, or maybe three."

"I wouldn't drink too much before the party if I were you."

"I know you wouldn't. That's because you are a stronger character than I. You are not I, however, which is your good luck, and it doesn't matter about the party, anyhow, because I have decided not to go."

"Not go to the party? Why?"

"Must I have a reason? Very well. I'll give you several and you can take your pick. I hate the club. I hate your sickening friends. I hate dull parties. I just prefer to stay at home. Is any of those satisfactory?"

"I think you are being unreasonable."

"Do you? No doubt I am."

"It would be different if you were ill."

"Is that what you want me to say? All right, I'm ill. I'm ill and can't go to the party. That's what I had planned to tell you, anyhow, and it would have been simpler if I had done it to begin with."

He was silent for so long a time that she turned her head and looked at him, and she was surprised to see that his face was deathly white with the mouth so distorted that it looked like an ugly, ragged wound. She realized that he was very angry and was controlling himself by a monstrous exertion of will. She had never seen him angry before, and she felt suddenly a stirring of excitement, almost a sense of exhilaration. After a moment, he stepped forward deliberately and slapped her across the face. It was a strong blow that knocked her head around and would have sent her sprawling from the chair if the arm had not prevented it. Her glass dropped from her hand and rolled across the carpet, leaving a trail of wetness and spread slowly through the pile.

"I will tell you something," he said. "You will go to the party to-night."

The blow struck, the excitement was gone. In its place was utter acceptance of the inevitable in the belief that nothing could ever have been different from what it had been and nothing could be changed from what it was bound to be. She was a fool ever to have thought otherwise. The bad day was going and the worse night was coming, and she had survived the one in order to fulfill her commitment to the other. So much was quite simple and quite true. She leaned her head back against the chair and closed her eyes.

"All right," she said. "If you want me to go, I will go."

SECTION 2

The Corinth Country Club hired a live orchestra every Saturday night. Once in a while, for something special, it was an orchestra from Midland City, and sometimes it was even one of the name bands you had probably heard on radio or had at home on platters, but usually it was the Corinth High Flyers, which it was tonight. Besides the piano, there were six instruments in the orchestra, seven if you counted both the saxophone and the clarinet, which were played at different times by the same Flyer, and people were always saying that it didn't make much sense to lay out all that money for an outside organization when you had something just as good or better right at home. The girl vocalist was good too, a damn sight better than most of the girls up in big time, and it was just one of those things that she wasn't up there herself, but of course everyone knew that the breaks made all the difference in that sort of success, and for each one who made it there were at least a dozen just as good who didn't. The vocalist was billed as Flame Farrell, a platinum blonde whose name alluded to temperament and not pigmentation. According to Merlin Collins, who claimed to have learned from experience, her temperament could be incited to fever heat by the sight of a twenty-dollar bill.

In Merlin Collins' opinion, virility was an obligation. His own was uncertain, as a matter of fact, and he was therefore constantly trying to prove that it wasn't by attempting to seduce as many women as possible, preferably the wives of his friends in order to give them an idea of what they were missing in their routine engagements. It was part of his technique to call all women baby. Take the average woman at the right time, he always said, you could do almost anything with her if you called her baby. They all liked it, every damn one of them, even the ones who pretended they didn't, and the ones who liked it most were the ones who were getting a little older than they liked to admit. Like the one old Avery Lawes had picked up in Miami, for instance. Chances were she was pushing thirty, and she tried to act like she was in cold storage or something, but, by God, she was a damn attractive woman in a snotty kind of way, and that was the kind that surprised you. The reserved ones, that was. It was really something to see the way the reserved ones fell apart in the end, all of a sudden with a God-damn bang, and there was always a fire inside. That was why they always acted so cold and snotty, of course, because they knew the fire was there and had to be watched all the time to keep it from getting out of control.

The night had been bad from the beginning, just as Lisa had known it would be, and it kept getting worse as the party progressed, which was true only because it was part of the pattern of degeneration and not because of any particular pressure the party itself imposed. Actually, it was a very casual party, and Lisa's obligations as hostess were practically nil. Three tables had been pushed together to accommodate the guests in a group and to serve as a base of operations, and once the guests had been greeted and orientated, it was mostly no more than a matter of letting them alone to operate, and of picking up the tab afterward, which was Avery's concern and not hers. Emerson and Ed Page had not yet come, however, late as it was, and this disturbed her and aroused in her an unreasonable fury, because it was perfectly apparent that they were delaying their arrival in order to deprive her as long as possible of the only pleasure she might have in the party, which was at best a masochistic pleasure, and it was even possible that Emerson had lied to hurt her, had promised that he would come and bring Ed when he really had no intention of doing so at all. She began to curse them silently, calling them in her mind the vilest names she could think of, and when at last she saw them enter the room and come toward the tables, all the strength that had been shored by anger ran out of her like so much water, leaving her drained and depleted and a little ill.

Avery had also seen Emerson and Ed enter, and he went to meet them and escort them to the table, and she understood that he had been watching for them and was anxious to make them feel welcome and at ease in company that was new to them. He started introducing them to the people who were present at that moment, and Lisa watched and waited as they approached her place, and as she waited she listened with accustomed ears to the thin, despairing cry of her desire in the wasteland of her heart. In Ed tonight there was more than loveliness. There was awareness of loveliness, and a pride in it, a conscious assumption of pride made essential by shyness and the necessity to assure herself that she had nothing to fear or to feel ashamed of. And above all, though she didn't know it, she was the siren of the shining, deadly island, a high, sweet voice in lotus-laden air.

They reached Lisa finally, and Avery said, "Here are Ed and Em, Lisa."

She looked up at them and hated them because they had caused her anguish and were causing her anguish now and weren't even sensitive enough to know it, and she thought that it would be much better and easier to bear if only they knew or were capable of knowing.

"I had given up," she said coldly. "I thought you weren't coming."

Emerson looked apologetic. "Because we're late? We're sorry about that. We had trouble getting away at the last moment."

"It doesn't matter. It was inconsiderate of me to invite you in the first place. You will probably find it a very dull party and wish that you had stayed away."

"I'm sure we won't. I'm sure we'll enjoy ourselves."

"Are you, really? I must say I doubt that very much. I find it impossible to believe that anyone could enjoy one of our parties. However, now that you are here, you might as well try. Why don't you have a drink the very first thing? I find that it helps if you start drinking immediately. And you mustn't stop. Whatever you do, you mustn't stop."

Avery laughed. "That's what I call good advice. I think we could make almost anything out of the stuff on the table here. What will you have?"

"A martini?" Ed said.

"Certainly. How about you, Em?"

"That's good for me too, but couldn't we make them ourselves?"

"Not the first one. After this, you're on your own."

He made the martinis and poured them and handed them to Ed and Emerson.

"As you can see, this is pretty casual," he said. "People just wander off and wander back. I hope you don't mind."

"Of course not." Emerson tasted the martini and found it below Roscoe's average. He turned to Ed. "Would you like to dance, honey?"

"I'll finish this first. Perhaps Lisa will dance with you."

Lisa shook her head and said coldly, "No, thank you. I don't think I care to dance."

At the other end of the room the High Flyers quit playing one tune and began playing another.

Avery excused himself and went off to see about something.

Emerson and Ed finished their martinis and went off to dance.

Almost everyone finished something and went off to start something.

Except Lisa. Lisa sat in a posture of primness and listened to the crying of her desire.

And at the time that must have been established for it, Merlin came and sat down in the chair beside her.

She looked at him with a feeling of contempt and revulsion, and she would certainly have got up and walked away if she had known that he was the catalyst that would change despair to ruin, but this was something she did not know nor even suspect. In fact, she was achieving gradually a precarious remission of emotional tension and was beginning to regret her rudeness to Avery and to Emerson and Ed, and she was thinking that surely she could wear out the rest of the terrible party with superficial friendliness at least.

And so she smiled and said, "Avery's gone off to see about something. Everyone else is dancing, I think."

"Except you and me, baby."

He used the two personal pronouns with a nuance of intimacy that made her flesh crawl, as if he had created an improper understanding between them merely by speaking the words in conjunction, but she only smiled again, feeling inordinately proud of her ability to do it, and lifted the glass she had been holding with the fingers of one hand.

"That's right, of course," she said. "Except you and me.

"You like to dance with old Merlin?"

"Oh, I don't think so. Do you mind?"

"No. Rather not dance myself, to tell the truth. Don't care much for dancing. Consider it a waste of time."

He laughed windily and wetly, blowing a fine spray. Some of the spittle struck her cheek, and she jerked her free hand up automatically to wipe it away. He was quite drunk, however, and did not notice either his offense or her reaction. His face was flaccid, the skin loose and ugly under his eyes, the muscles sagging at the corners of his mouth. Fumbling a case out of his pocket, he offered her a cigarette. She took the cigarette and put it between her lips, and he found his lighter after a short search and provided flame. She pulled smoke through the tobacco and into her lungs in an acrid and soothing cloud, creating on the cigarette a bright red head.

"How about a little air?" he said. "Hot in here, don't you think?"

"It's hotter outside."

"Oh. Guess so, at that. No air-conditioning outside. Have to think of a better excuse. Let me see, let me see. Got it. Darker outside. How's that? Tempted? Does its being darker outside suggest any advantages over being inside?"

"None that I can think of."

"Really? Old Avery must be neglecting your training. Suspected as much, to tell you the truth. If you don't mind my saying so, you've got a frustrated look. Damn shame. Beautiful women shouldn't be frustrated. Come on, baby. Let old Merlin unfrustrate you. Greatest little unfrustrater around."

He leaned forward abruptly, and she felt the minor trespassing of his hand under the table, and then there was a shrill scream of pain, like a woman's scream, and he was standing on his feet with his chair turned over behind him and one hand clapped to his cheek and tears running out of his eyes, and in the eyes were fear and a kind of foolish incredulity, and he kept saying over and over with a bubbling sound, "Oh, Jesus, Jesus, Jesus," and she understood after a moment, though she could never remember the action specifically, that she had thrust the red coal of her cigarette into his face.

Everyone was looking at them, naturally, everyone arrested and fixed in a terrible tableau, and even the High Flyers trailed raggedly to silence in the realization that something had happened and was terribly wrong. Then Merlin turned and ran out of the room with an awkward, loping gait, still holding his seared cheek and whimpering with pain and saying Jesus, Jesus over and over, and someone who turned out to be Avery detached himself from the fixed members of the tableau, and right away the tableau began to break and move in its many parts, and the High Flyers began to play again, and everyone started pretending that nothing had happened. And Avery approached Lisa in the desolate ruins of the worse night that had become worst.

"For Christ's sake, what have you done?" he said.

"It seems that I have burned the cheek of Merlin Collins with a cigarette."

"Why? Can you possibly tell me why?"

"Because he is a fool and deserved it."

"Are you in a position to condemn fools? Anyhow, that is no reason for doing a thing like that."

"Isn't it? Then I did it for no reason."

"I insist on knowing why you did it, Lisa."

"I have told you the reason. If you don't believe me, you had better ask Merlin."

"I shall. I shall also ask him to forgive you for what you have done, though God knows why he should."

"You may do as you wish. First, however, I would like to go home."

"It's impossible. I have guests. I can't take you home now."

"I will not stay here any longer. I didn't want to come, and you compelled me, and now I will not stay any longer."

She could see that he was angry again, as he had been at home in the living room, and she thought that the only reason he did not strike her now, as he had then, was that they were now exposed to the public. His anger did not disturb her. She regretted a little, perhaps, that she was causing him so much trouble, for she felt sincerely that he did not deserve it, but it was quite evident by now that the trouble was inevitable, something to which she was party but over which she had absolutely no control, and so the regret was really futile and not worth expressing.

Standing, she said, "I'll go outside to the car. If you want to come, you can come. If not, it doesn't matter." She walked across the room and outside, and it was quite a long walk with everyone watching her, the kind of situation that would usually make your arms and legs go in all directions at once, but she felt strangely at ease, not in the conviction that the worst of the night had passed, but in the serenity of resignation to progressive: evil, and she walked gracefully with her head back and her slight body erect. She went to the parking area and got into the front seat of Avery's black Caddy and sat there with her eyes closed, and after quite a while a man came and got in beside her. The man was not Avery, but she knew instantly without opening her eyes just who he was, and she began to laugh quietly with the merest whisper of sound because it was so perfectly part of the pattern that he should be who he was.

"Avery didn't want to leave his guests," Emerson said. "He asked me to drive you home. Do you object?"

"It would not matter if I did. You would still drive me home."

"If you prefer, I'll tell Avery to ask someone else."

"No. It was necessary that he ask you and that you should agree."

"Why do you say that? I don't understand you."

"Don't you? Perhaps it's just as well."

He backed the Caddy out of its position between two other cars and drove out of the parking area.

"Didn't you drive Avery home from your place one night?" she said.

"Yes. A long time back."

"I know. In November. The night before he left for Miami. I disgraced myself tonight, didn't I? Everyone will be talking about it. It was a very beautiful public spectacle, wasn't it?"

"I don't know, Lisa."

"Of course you know. How ridiculous to say you don't. You were there and saw it all quite clearly. Do you know why I burned that fool's cheek with my cigarette?"

"Knowing Merlin, I can imagine."

"Because he pawed me? He did that, of course, but it wasn't the real reason. It was just a kind of precipitant. Would you care to know the real reason?"

"No."

"Are you sure? I'm just in the mood for telling you if you'd like to know."

"I'm quite sure."

"Oh, very well. Be as smug as you like. Do you know that you are very smug?"

"I don't try to be."

"Of course you don't try. It just comes naturally. Because you are a nice guy who does things. That's what you are. A nice, smug guy who does things."

"I'm sorry you find me so unpleasant."

"You say that you're sorry, but you're not. You don't care at all. You don't care because you despise me."

"I don't despise you, Lisa."

"Certainly you despise me. Shall I tell you why? You despise me because I'm despicable. That's very logical, isn't it? How can you deny anything as logical as that?" She was very pleased with this. She had reasoned logically and confounded him completely. She began to laugh again quietly to herself, continuing to sit with her head back and her eyes closed, and it wasn't long before she was aware that the Caddy had stopped, and then she opened her eyes and saw that they were parked in the car port beside the house.

"Here we are," Emerson said. "I'll see you to the door."

She looked at him slyly. "Won't you come in for a drink?"

"No, thanks, Lisa. I don't think I'd better."

"You see? I said you despise me, and you do. You won't even come in for a drink when I ask you. It would only be common courtesy to come in for a drink."

"God damn it, I do not despise you. I like you very much. I just think it would not be a good idea to come in for a drink."

"Why? Are you afraid I would seduce you?"

"Certainly not."

"Would you be surprised if I tried?"

"I don't think you are going to."

"Why? Do you think I am incapable? Is that what you think?"

"I don't think anything about it at all."

"Perhaps you don't trust yourself. Is that it? Are you afraid you could not resist?"

"All right, Lisa. Perhaps that's it. Anyhow, whatever it is, I am not coming in for either a drink or a seduction, and I will take you to the door and no farther."

"No. Wait a minute."

He had started to open the door beside him, and now he paused and turned back toward her in the seat, and she moved suddenly with incredible speed and was upon him in an instant, her mouth over his mouth and her body pressing against his body, but he was of course only the necessary medium, and the mouth and the body she sought were not his nor even present, and in her was the wild, aberrant unleashed hunger, and her harsh whisper in her throat had a strangled, dying sound.

"Here," she whispered. "Right here, right now."

He sat passively under the attack, neither resisting nor responding, thinking that she would soon withdraw, but she continued to press upon him and devour him, and he began to think that he himself would surely strangle and die. Raising his hands to her wrists, he tried to break her grip but couldn't, and so he took the fingers of her hands and pried them loose and pushed her away from him. Then he opened the door and got out quickly and went around the car and opened the opposite door. She was now sitting quietly in the seat with her hands folded in her lap, and he felt for her a deep, bitter pity that was like nothing he had ever felt before.

"Come on, Lisa. Let me take you to the door."

She got out and started to walk toward the front of the car, but when he took a step after her, she stopped and whirled around with that incredible and savage speed, her voice a thin projection of venom that shocked him and made him feel suddenly withered and sick.

"Go away! Go away at once before I kill you!"

Turning, she went on alone around the car and up across the porch and into the front hall. She stood just inside the door and listened to the Caddy's motor start and diminish and die away, and whatever it was that had been waiting in the house all day and had been waiting when she had left the house at the end of the day was still waiting now that she had returned to the house in the middle of the night. She stood there for a few minutes, wondering where she should go and what she should do, and then she walked into the living room and turned on a light and began walking slowly around the room, stopping and looking at things and picking them up and setting them down again. After a while she came to a console radio-phonograph that was hardly ever used by anyone, and she got down on her knees and began to look through the records in the cabinet, and after she had looked at perhaps a dozen she came to one called *Death and Transfiguration*. She remained on her knees in a posture of prayer, looking at the label on the record and thinking that she had tried in a way to achieve a transfiguration, and it had not worked, it had only gone from bad to worse to worst, and perhaps after all death was the only transfiguration, the only possible real change, and anyhow this would surely be a solacing record to listen to in the ruins of this worst of all nights. Getting up from her knees, she put the record on the machine and sat down to listen to it, and she found in the music a great and cathedral-like gloom that was tremendously satisfying. When the record was finished, she sat still and permitted the mechanism to start it playing again, and she continued to sit still and listen while the machine repeated the record a number of times, and one of the remarkable things about it was that in all this time, which was considerable, she didn't even seem to want a drink. Not until the Caddy came back into the drive did she get up and stop the machine and go upstairs. In her room, she took off her dress and her shoes and lay down on the bed in darkness and listened to the small sounds involved in the elimination of time and space between her and Avery, his entrance into the house, his ascent of the stairs, his entrance into the room, his sigh as he sat on the edge of her bed.

"Lisa," he said.

"Yes?"

"How are you feeling?"

"I am feeling quite well, thank you."

"Are you? I'm glad that one of us is feeling well, at least, because I am not. I am feeling tired and defeated. I feel as if I had come to the end of things."

"It's my fault. I'm sorry, but I can't help it. Once I could have helped it, and I should have done it then, but you can see that now it is much too late."

"Yes, I can see that. I see it and accept it. Did you mind my asking Em to bring you home?"

"No, I didn't mind, but it would have been better if you hadn't. I tried to seduce him and was unsuccessful."

"Why on earth did you do that? I don't understand."

"Because he is a man and I am what I am? The answer is very simple. It wasn't him at all. It was someone else. Now do you understand?"

"I think that I do. As nearly as it is possible for me to understand."

"It is certainly devious, isn't it? Perhaps you think it is unnatural. Do I disgust you?"

"No."

"Certainly I must disgust you. And you must also certainly hate me. I will feel better about it if you hate me."

"I told you that I am tired and defeated. I am much too tired to feel disgust or hatred or anything else. I can't even feel disgust or hatred for myself, which is something that has not been true since I was a small boy."

He got up slowly from the edge of the bed and went out of the room, and she lay in the silence he left behind and did not move. In time he came back and sat down again on the bed, and something hard lay lightly on the bone above her heart.

"Do you know what this is?" he said.

"It feels like a gun."

"That's what it is. A gun. Do you know what I am thinking?"

"You are thinking that you will kill me."

"Would you mind a great deal if I were to kill you?"

"I don't think so. I have often wanted to die, and once I tried, and I think I would be grateful if you killed me now."

"Do you remember what I said when you asked me the last time why I wanted you to stay?"

"Yes, I remember."

"What did I say?"

"That if our marriage was not the beginning of something good, it should at least be the end of everything bad."

"That's right. That's what I said."

"Are you going to kill me?"

"I don't know yet. I'm thinking about it."

He thought about it, and she lay with the weight above her heart and listened alone to the dry interior weeping, the vestige of impossible tears.

CHAPTER VII

And it ends, as it began, with Emerson Page, a nice guy who never quite knew what it was all about.

He lay beside Ed, lying very still so as not to disturb her, and he tried to figure it in his mind, how it had started and grown and come at last to the end it had come to, but it made no sense to him whatever, it would never make any sense to him as long as he lived, and what disturbed him profoundly, in addition to the sorrow he felt as a compassionate man, was the thought that he might himself have been in some measure responsible. He knew in his heart that this was not so, that it could not possibly be so, but there was still to remember the horror of last night, her savage attack that seemed now in retrospect to have been a supplication, and the final venomous words that were the last he would ever hear from her and that he now heard like an echo above the breathing of Ed.

He listened to the voice and the breathing, and he was grateful for Ed's warm body so near him, but for some strange reason he did not want to touch her or have any physical contact with her at all, and this was the first time he had ever felt such a reluctance. It was something that would soon pass, he knew that very well, but at this moment it existed for the first time, and he would not have thought it possible.

He could not sleep, and he wanted a cigarette, and he wondered if he could get up and get one without disturbing Ed. Very carefully, he swung his legs over the side of the bed and sat up on the edge, and he was immediately aware, even before she spoke, that Ed was not asleep and had not been asleep, but had been lying quietly, like him, staring up into the darkness.

"You're still thinking about it," she said.

"I know. I can't help it. Both of them that way. Shooting her and then himself."

"Darling, you had better forget it."

"Can *you* forget it?"

"No, but it would be better if I could."

"I keep wondering why."

"Darling, you had better quit wondering."

"There was something wrong between them, Ed. I keep thinking I might have helped."

"You know what was wrong between them, and there was no way you could have helped."

"I guess so. I guess you're right. Would you care for a cigarette?"

"No, thanks."

He got up and found one for himself and lit it and went out of the bedroom into the living room and across the living room to the front window. He stood there smoking the cigarette and looking down into the street of Corinth, and the street was narrow and lifeless and splotched with dirty light, and he remembered it suddenly as he had seen it three-quarters of a year ago with the snow slanting out of the night and a strong wind blowing between the buildings. It seemed to him that everything had begun that night, the whole sad and confusing business of Avery Lawes and the woman who had become Lisa Lawes briefly and to no good purpose, but he knew that this could not really be true, that nothing actually began and ended in so short a time. All things come from many times and sources, and there is no short and simple chronology to the bad end.

The smoke of the cigarette was hot and harsh in his throat and lungs. He finished it and went back to the bed and lay down beside Ed with the space between them.

"Roscoe and I drank a toast to them," he said. "Good bedding, good breeding, good fortune. I guess they didn't have any of it."

"Don't keep thinking, darling."

"Roscoe said I was worried about Avery. He said it; was like I was afraid he'd never have the good luck I wished him."

"Don't, darling."

"What could a man do but wish?"

"Please don't, darling."

He reached over and put his hand flat on her warm thigh, and her arm crossed his in a duplicate gesture, and nothing that was wrong became right, but everything that had been right was still right and would always be. They lay in the warm intimacy of mutual appeal and acceptance, and the dark room was again, or still, because of them and what they were and felt, one of Earth's good places.

Eventually they slept.

THE WITNESS
WAS A LADY

It was a Thursday morning when Corey McDown called me. I hadn't heard from Corey for a long time. Not directly. After he got to be a cop, we sort of drifted apart and lost contact with each other. I'm not exactly allergic to cops, you understand, but it usually turns out that we're incompatible.

Corey was a bright guy, and he'd moved up fast in the force. He was pretty young for a lieutenant in Homicide.

"Hello, Mark," he said. "Corey McDown here. Did I get you out of bed?"

"I don't have to get out of bed to answer the phone," I said. "How are you, Corey?"

"I've been worse," he said, "and I've been better. I wonder if you'd do me a favor."

"Do I owe you a favor?"

"Do this one for me, and I'll owe *you* one."

"You think I may need it?"

"You may, Mark. You never know."

"True. There have been times before. What's on your mind, Corey?"

"I hate long telephone conversations. Ask me over."

"Sure, Corey. Come on over."

"Give me thirty minutes."

He hung up, and so did I. It must be a big favor he wanted, I thought, to make him so accommodating. I had an uneasy feeling that it was related to something that I didn't want to think about, and I wished I could quit. I got out of bed and shaved and showered and dressed, which used up the thirty minutes. I had just finished when the door buzzer sounded, and I went out across the living room to the door and opened it.

"Right on time," I said. "Come on in."

He came in and tossed his hat into one chair and sat down in another. His hair was cut short, a thick brown stubble, and he looked trim and hard. Right now, leaning back and smiling, relaxed.

"You've got a nice place, Mark. You live well."

"Heels always live well. It's expected of them."

"You're not a heel, Mark. You're just a reasonably good guy with kinks."

"Thanks." I walked over to a table and lifted a glass. "You want some breakfast?"

"Out of a bottle?"

"Is there another place to get it?"

"I had mine out of a skillet. You go ahead."

I poured a double shot of bourbon and swallowed it fast. Then I went back and threw his hat on the floor and took its place. The double helped me feel as relaxed as he looked.

"Go on," I said. "Convince me."

"Don't rush me. I'm trying to think of the best approach."

"The best is the simplest. You want a favor. Tell me what it is."

"Let me ask you a question first. You seen Nora lately?"

"No. It's been forever. Why?"

"I thought you might have looked her up when Jack Kirby was murdered."

"I didn't."

"That's strange. Old friends and all, I mean. The least an old friend can do when an old friend's boy friend is killed is to offer sympathy and condolences and all that."

"My personal opinion is that congratulations were in order. I didn't think it would be in good taste to offer them."

He looked across at me, shaking his burr head and grinning. The grin got vocal and became a loud laugh.

"You see, Mark? All you've got are a few kinks. A real twenty-four carat heel like Jack Kirby offends your sensibilities."

"Go to hell."

"Sure, sure. Anything to oblige. What I'm leading up to is, this favor isn't really for me at all. Oh, incidentally it is, maybe, but mostly it's a favor for Nora."

"You sound like a man about to be devious, Corey."

"Not me, Mark. Whatever I may be that makes me different from you, I'm not devious. I haven't got the brains for it."

"O.K. Tell me the favor for Nora that's one for you incidentally."

"I'll tell you, but let's get the circumstances in focus. Did you read the news stories about Jack Kirby's murder?"

"Once over, lightly."

"In that case, you'll remember what the evidence indicated. He had an appointment with someone in his apartment. At least someone came to see him there, and this someone, whoever it was, killed him. Cracked his skull with a heavy cut-glass decanter, to be exact. This was all in the news stories, and it's all true. What wasn't in the stories, because we put the lid on it, is that someone pretty definitely knew who it was in the apartment with Kirby that night. That someone is Nora."

"How do you know?"

"Never mind how. We know."

"That won't do, Corey. You can't expect to clam up on the guy you're asking for a favor."

"All right. I'll tell you this much. The day of Kirby's murder, Nora told a friend that she was going to Kirby's apartment that night, but she couldn't go until late because Kirby was expecting someone earlier that she didn't want to meet. This friend is a woman whose testimony can be relied on. We're convinced of that."

"Didn't Nora mention the name of Kirby's expected guest?"

"No. No name. Just that it was someone she didn't want to meet there."

"Did you ask Nora?"

Corey looked down at his hands in his lap. He folded and unfolded the blunt fingers. On his face for a few seconds there was a sour expression as he recalled an experience that he hadn't liked and couldn't forget.

"We hauled her in and asked her over and over for a long while. She wouldn't say. She denied ever having told her friend that she knew."

"I wonder why. You'd think she'd want to help."

"Come off it, Mark. You know why as well as I do. Jack Kirby was a guy who associated with dangerous characters. One of these characters killed him, and he wouldn't think twice about killing a material witness. Either to keep her from talking or in revenge if she did. If he couldn't do it personally, he'd have it done for him. Today or tomorrow or next year. Nora's been associating with some dangerous characters herself, including Kirby. She knows how they operate, Mark. She won't talk because she's afraid."

"Well, Nora's not exactly a strong personality. She'll break eventually. Why don't you ask her again?"

"I wish I could."

"Why can't you? Like you said, she's a material witness. You can arrest her and hold her."

"I could if I could get hold of her." He looked down at his hands again, at the flexing fingers. His face was smooth and hard now, the sour expression dissolved. "I should have held her when I had her, but that was my mistake. A man makes lots of mistakes for old times' sake."

"Asking and giving favors, you mean. That sort of thing."

"Maybe. We'll see."

"Speaking of favors, where do I come in? If you think I know where Nora is, you're wrong."

"That's not the problem. I already know where she is."

"In that case, why don't you pick her up?"

"Because she's across the state line. You may know that we don't have any extradition agreement with our neighbor covering material witnesses."

"I didn't know, as a matter of fact. Thanks for telling me. It may come in handy. I don't seem to remember reading any of this about Nora in the papers."

"I told you. It wasn't there. We've kept the lid on it. The point is, we can't keep the lid on any longer. The story's going to break in the evening editions, and that's what worries me."

"I can see why. You won't look so good, letting a material witness slip away from you. Tough. You expect me to bleed, Corey?"

"It's not that. I'll survive a little criticism. It's Nora I'm worried about."

"Old times' sake again?"

"Call it what you like, but you can see her position. She's a constant and deadly threat to Jack Kirby's killer, whoever he is, and the moment the story breaks, the killer is going to know it. He'll also know where to find her."

"I see what you mean. The threat works two ways."

"That's it. And that's where you come in."

"Don't tell me. You want me to go and talk to her and convince her that she's got to come back and turn herself in for her own good."

"You're a smart guy, Mark. You always were."

"Sure. With kinks. To tell you the truth, I'm not quite convinced that this mysterious visitor of Kirby's is going to be so desperate as you imagine."

"You think he won't? Why?"

"Well, Nora knows he was supposed to be at Kirby's at a certain time. At the time Kirby was killed. So she knows. That's not absolute proof that he was actually there. Even if he was there, it's not proof that he did the killing. It's a lead, Corey, not a conviction."

"A lead's all we need. The visitor killed Kirby. We're certain of it. Once we know who he was, we'll find more evidence fast enough. We'll know what to look for, and how and where to find it."

"You haven't told me yet where Nora is."

"About a hundred miles from here. The first place I thought to check. The natural place for a woman to run when she's scared and in trouble."

"Home?"

"What used to be. Down on the farm."

"Regression, as the psychs say. You were sharp to think of that right off the bat, Corey. You're quite a psych yourself."

He got up suddenly and walked over to a pair of matched windows overlooking a small court in which, below, there was some green stuff growing.

He stood there looking out for a minute or more, and then he turned and walked back but did not sit down again.

"You and Nora were always close, Mark, back there when we were kids. Closer than ever Nora and I were. I used to hate you for that, but it doesn't matter any longer. It's one of the things I've gotten over. The point is, she'll be in danger. I believe that or I wouldn't be here. She wouldn't listen to me, but she might to you. Will you go talk to her?"

"Why should I?"

"Do you have to have the reasons spelled out?"

"I can't think of any."

"As a favor for me?"

"I don't want to obligate you."

"For Nora, then?"

"Nora wants me to leave her alone. She told me so."

"Not even to save her life?"

"Nora's a big girl now. She associates with dangerous characters and makes up her own mind."

He stood looking down at me, his face as bleak and empty as a department store floorwalker's. Turning away, he picked his hat off the floor and held it by the brim in his hands.

"I guess those kinks are bigger than I thought," he said.

He went over to the door and let himself out, and I kept on sitting in the chair, thinking about a time that he'd recalled. She used to ride into town to high school on the school bus, Nora did. Corey and I were town boys. We were snobbish with the country kids until we met Nora, who was a country kid, and then we weren't snobbish any more. She was slim and lovely and seemed to move with incredible grace in a kind of golden haze. She was so lovely, in fact, that she intimidated me for almost a full year before we finally got together on a picnic one Sunday afternoon. After that, I began to know Nora as she was—as a touchable and lusty little manipulator, almost amoral, who already had, even then, certain carefully conceived and directed ideas about what Nora wanted out of life. I didn't love her any the less, maybe more, but I resigned myself to the obvious truth that I was no more at most than a kind of privileged expedient.

After high school, Nora and Corey and I drifted at different times across the hundred miles to the city. At first we saw each other now and then, but later hardly at all. Corey became a cop. Thanks to luck and cards and certain contacts, I learned to live well without excessive effort. As for Nora—well, I had just refused to do her a favor at Corey's request, but there had been plenty of others to do her favors, as there always are with girls like her, and some of the favors came to five figures. Jack Kirby had not been the first. Maybe he would be the last.

I stood up and walked over to the windows and looked down into the court, down at the green stuff growing. I wasn't used to the radiance of day, and the light seemed intensely bright, and it hurt my eyes. My head ached, and I wondered if I could stand another double shot, or even a single, but I decided that I couldn't. Turning away from the windows, I walked back across the living room and into the soft and seductive dusk of the bedroom. I lay down on the unmade bed and tried to think with some kind of orderliness, and the thinking must have been therapeutic, for after a while I lost the headache, or became unaware of it.

Granted, I thought, that Nora knew the identity of Jack Kirby's visitor, who was also Jack Kirby's killer. Corey was convinced that she did, and Corey was a bright guy. Being a bright guy, it was funny how he could go so far wrong from a good start. It was funny, a real scream, but I didn't feel like laughing. Because she'd refused to talk, because she'd run and hid to escape the pressure that would certainly have broken her down, Corey assumed that she was afraid of the consequences of pointing a finger, the vengeance of a killer or a killer's hired hand, but it wasn't true. It couldn't be. She had run from the pressure, true, but she had kept her silence simply because she did not want Jack Kirby's visitor to be known. For old times' sake. It was touching, really, and I appreciated it.

I went over in my mind again with odd detachment, as if I were reviewing an experience of someone else, the way it had happened that I had killed Jack Kirby. I hadn't intended to, although it was a pleasure when I did, and all I'd actually intended when I went up to his apartment that night was to pay an overdue debt of a couple of grand.

I had lost the two grand to Kirby in a stud game that proved to be the beginning of a streak of bad luck. In the first place, to show how bad my luck was beginning to be, I lost the pot on three of a kind, which is pretty difficult to do in straight stud. In the second place, to show how fast bad luck can get worse in a streak, I didn't have the two grand. All I had to offer was an IOU with a twenty-four-hour deadline. The deadline passed, and I still didn't have the two grand. My intentions were good, but my luck kept on being bad. I got three extensions on the deadline, and then I had a couple of visitors. They came to my apartment about the middle of the afternoon, a few minutes after I'd gotten out of bed. I'd seen both of them around, and I knew the name of one of them, but the names didn't matter. It was a business call, not social. They were very polite in a businesslike way. Only one of them talked.

"Mr. Sanders," he said, "we're representing Mr. Jack Kirby in a little business matter."

"Times have been tough," I said.

"Mr. Kirby appreciates that, but he feels that he's been more than liberal."

"Thank Mr. Kirby for me."

"I'm afraid Mr. Kirby wants more than thanks. He wants to know if you're prepared to settle your obligation."

"How about a payment on account? Ten percent, say."

"Sorry. Mr. Kirby feels that the obligation should be settled in full. He's prepared to extend your time until eight o'clock tomorrow night. He expects you to call at his apartment at that hour with the full amount due and payable."

"Tell Mr. Kirby I'll give the matter my careful attention."

"Mr. Kirby wants us particularly to remind you of the urgency."

"Fine. Consider me reminded."

"Mr. Kirby wants us to remind you in a manner that you will re-member." This was the clue to go to work, apparently, for that's what they did. I wasn't very alert yet, it being several hours until dark, and I put up what might be called a sorry defense. In fact, I didn't put up any defense at all. The mute suddenly had me from behind in a combination hammerlock and stranglehold, and the talker, looking apologetic, belted me three times in the belly. At the door, leaving me doubled up on the floor, the talker stopped and looked back, an expression of compassion spreading among the pocks on his flat face.

"Sorry, Mr. Sanders," he said. "Nothing personal, you understand."

I wasn't able to acknowledge the apology with the good grace it deserved. After they were gone, I began to breathe again, and a little later I successfully stood up. The beating had been painful, but not crippling.

It was a break in a way, the beating was. It was the nadir of the streak, the worst of the bad luck, and now that things had got about as bad as they could get, they began immediately to get better. What I mean is, I took the ten percent I'd offered Kirby's hired goons and ran it through another game of stud and brought it out multiplied by twenty. A little better than four grand in paper with not an IOU in the bundle. By midnight I had in my possession, as the talking goon had said, the full amount due and payable.

The next night at eight, I was at Kirby's door. I rang the bell, and Kirby let me in. He was wearing most of a tux, the exception being a maroon smoking jacket with a black satin sash. I happen to have an aversion to satin sashes, on smoking jackets or anything else, and this put me in a bad humor. It made it more difficult than ever to be reasonable about the beating he had bought for me. Apparently I was wearing nothing to which he had a comparable aversion. His long, sallow face, divided under a long nose by a long, thin moustache, was perfectly amiable.

"Hello, Mark," he said. "Glad to see you."

"Even broke?" I said.

"Sorry." His face lost its amiability. "Poverty depresses me."

"Never mind. I'm not one of your huddled masses. I come loaded."

"Good." The amiability was back. "I was sure you could manage if you really tried."

I took the ready bundle from a pocket, two grand exactly, and handed it to him. He transferred it to a pocket of his offending jacket with hardly more than a glance, and this put me in a worse humor than I was already in, which was bad enough. I knew he would count the money the moment I was gone, and it would have been less annoying if he had counted it honestly in front of me.

"Now I'll have the IOU, if you don't mind," I said.

"Certainly, Mark." He took the paper out of the same pocket the money had gone into. "I hope you don't resent the little reminder I was forced to send you."

"Not at all. It was very courteous and regretful, and it only hit me where it doesn't show."

"I'm glad you understand. Will you have a drink before you leave?"

"Bourbon and water."

"Good. I'll have one with you."

He turned and walked over to a liquor cabinet and worked for a minute with a bottle and glasses. "I'm sorry I can't ask you to stay for more than one, but I'm expecting company."

"Company's nice if it's nice company."

"This is nice. Someone you once knew, I believe. Nora Erskine? Charming girl. Beautiful. She has a very warm nature. Very generous."

He came toward me with a glass in each hand, and I hit him in the mouth. Don't ask me why. Maybe a disciple of Freud could tell you, but I can't. He fell backward in a shower of bourbon and came up with a little gun in his hand, which seemed to indicate that he hadn't been quite so amiable and trusting as he'd appeared. The cut-glass decanter was there on a table beside me, and I picked it up and smashed it over his head, and he fell down dying and was dead in less than a minute.

Stripped to the bone, that was how I killed him. I tried to remember if I had touched anything besides the decanter and the outside of the door, and there seemed to be nothing, and so I wiped the neck of the decanter with my handkerchief and retrieved the two grand, which was no good to him, and left. I went home and thought about it, wondering if I should leave town incognito, but I decided that there was no need. The goons knew that I was supposed to be at Kirby's, of course, but the goons were old pros. They'd done a job and were through with it. They couldn't care less that Jack Kirby had got himself killed. As a matter of fact, if they made the logical deduction, I would probably go up immeasurably in their regard. The result of my thinking was the decision that it was unnecessary to take any precipitate action. I only needed to proceed with caution, as the signs beside the highways say, in the direction I was going.

But that was then, and now was different. Now I knew that Nora knew, and Nora was not an old pro, and Nora would surely someday tell. Maybe not now or soon, but someday, the day she couldn't stand the pressure any longer, and the passage of time would not help or save me, for there is no statute of limitations on murder, not even murder which might turn out to be, with luck and a good lawyer, of lesser degree than first. And there was always the solid possibility, of course, of that grim first.

I could see that I had come to the time of decision now, and I didn't want to face it. Like many another in the same predicament, I found a way to avoid it temporarily, if not permanently. In any case it was simple. I simply went to sleep.

When I awoke again, it was evening, but the hour of the day was the only thing that had changed, not me or the problem or anything that had to be considered and done or not done. I got up and washed my face in cold water and put on a tie and jacket and went downstairs onto the street. There was a newsstand on the corner, half a block away, and I went down there and bought an evening edition and carried it back to the apartment without looking at it. In the apartment, I poured another double shot and drank half of it and sat down and opened the newspaper, and there was the story on page one: Material Witness in Kirby Slaying Flees State. I read the story slowly, finishing the second shot of the double as I read, and it was reported about the way Corey had told it to me in the morning, how Nora was believed to know the identity of Kirby's visitor at the time of the murder, and how she had refused to talk, and how, finally, she had escaped into the next state, from which she could not be extradited. It was also reported in the story exactly where she had gone and now was, the home of her childhood not more than a hundred miles away, and this was what I needed in order to make the decision I had to make, and you can see why. Now that her location was no longer a secret shared by me and the police, Nora was in greater danger and, as a consequence, so was I. There was therefore no longer any reason for indecision or delay, although there was probably no reason to hurry either.

I sat there for quite a long while, and it began to get dark outside in the city streets, and the incandescents and fluorescents and neons came on to drive the darkness back. I finally became aware, via my stomach, that I hadn't eaten all day, and that I had better eat something before I took another drink, which I wanted, and so I went out and had a steak in a restaurant down the street a few blocks. After eating, I walked back and had a couple more drinks in the apartment, and then I went down and got my car out of the garage in the basement and drove across town to a place where they were having a stud game. I won five hundred skins in the game, the good streak still running in the wake of the bad streak, and at some point in the time it took to win that much money, my mind made itself up and I knew what I was going to do. I dropped out of the game about three o'clock in the morning, a little after, and it was almost four when I got home.

In the bedroom of the apartment, I changed into slacks, sport shirt and jacket, heavier shoes. From a shelf in the closet I got a leather case that contained a .30-.30 rifle. I had been very good with a rifle when I was younger. There was no reason to believe that I wasn't still almost as good. I assembled the rifle and checked it and took it apart again. I put the parts back into the case and half a dozen cartridges into my jacket pocket. I don't know why I took so many, for chances were long that a dozen would not be enough if one wasn't. Carrying the case, I went back downstairs to my car and drove out of town.

It took me about three hours driving slowly, to reach the town where I had grown up a hundred years or so ago, and I did not drive into it after reaching it. Instead, I drove around it on roads I remembered, and beyond it on another road until I saw ahead of me, quite a distance and on the left, the white house of the Erskines. It sat rather far back from the road at the end of a tree-lined drive, though not so far as memory had it, and it had once been considered the finest farm home in the county, if not the state. Now it did not seem one-half so grand, a different house than I had known before, as if the first had been razed and a second built in its place in an identical design, with identical detail, but on a reduced scale.

I turned off before I reached the house, along the side of a country square. The road descended slowly for a quarter of a mile to a steel and timber bridge across a shallow ravine. There had been water in the ravine in the spring, and there would be water again when the fall rains came, but now the bed was dry except for intermittent shallow pools caught in rock. After crossing the bridge, I pulled off the road on a narrow turning into high weeds and brush. Getting out of the car, carrying the rifle case, I climbed a barbed-wire fence and followed the course of the ravine through a stand of timber, mostly oaks and maples and elms, and across a wide expanse of pasture in which a herd of Holsteins were having breakfast. Pretty soon I left the ravine and cut across two fields at an angle and up a long rise into a grove of walnut trees on the crest. I stopped among the trees and assembled and loaded the rifle, and then I lay down and looked down the slope on the other side of the crest to the house where Nora was supposed to be. There was a stone terrace on this side of the house at the rear. On the terrace was a round table and several brightly striped canvas chairs. Wide glass doors led off the terrace into the house. No one was visible from where I lay under the walnut trees about fifty yards away.

After half an hour, I rolled over onto my back and lay looking up into the branches of the trees where the green walnuts hung, and I began to remember all the times I'd come here to gather the nuts when I was a kid, sometimes with Nora in the later years. We gathered them in burlap bags—gunny sacks, they were called—and later knocked the blackened husks off with a hammer. For a long time afterward, if we didn't wear gloves, our hands were stained with the juice of the husks, a stain like the stain of nicotine, and there was no way to get this stain off except to wear it off, and you could always tell the ones who had gathered walnuts late in the fall by the stain on their hands that wore on toward winter.

I could hear a cow bell jangling back in the pasture. I could hear a dog barking. I could hear the cawing of a crow above the fields, and I thought I could hear, closing my eyes, the slow beating of his black wings against the still air. Opening my eyes, I rolled over and looked down the slope again to the terrace, and there was Nora standing beside the table and looking up toward the walnut grove as if she could see me lying in its shadow. She was wearing a white blouse and brown shorts, and her face and arms and legs were golden in the morning light. Drawing the rifle up along my side into firing position, I had her heart in my sights in a second, and I had a notion that it was a golden heart pumping golden blood.

She must have stood there for a full minute without moving, maybe longer, and then she turned and walked across the terrace and through the glass doors into the house, and I lowered my face slowly into the sweet green grass. I could still hear the bell and the dog and the crow, and I could hear the voice of Corey McDown saying that Mark Sanders was just a guy with kinks.

After a while I stood up and went back across the fields to the ravine and along the ravine through the pasture and the woods to the car. Driving to the city, I thought about what I had better do, and where I had better go, and how long it would take to learn to live comfortably with a constant threat, and I decided, although there was probably no hurry, that I might as well get my affairs in order and get somewhere a long way off as soon as possible.